WORLD SERIES ROOKIE

WORLD SERIES ROOKIE

by C. PAUL JACKSON

with drawings by Ralph E. Ricketts

Hastings House · Publishers · New York

CONTENTS

WORLD SERIES ROOKIE

CHAPTER ONE

Stub Alison, Big Leaguer

"Back to the high-school league, you sawed-off false alarm!"

A leather-lunged fan bellowed the crack as the inning ended and the Goliath players jogged off the diamond. Frank "Stub" Alison, two days past eighteen years of age and less than two weeks graduated from high school, felt his ears burn. He started toward the Goliath dugout at a pace considerably faster than a trot, but it seemed the longest distance he had ever covered on a ball field.

Goliath fans were not a bit backward in expressing their disapproval. Others joined the energetic shouter.

"How'd you get by even in a high-school league? . . . Little Leaguers handle line drives better than you, Alison! . . . The idea is for a big-league fielder to gauge that little white round thing and latch onto it! . . . They ought to give you a net instead of a glove, busher! . . ."

The journey from left field was misery all the way for the stubby youngster. And just an inning and a half ago, when the Goliath manager gruffly informed him that he was playing today, he had been—in his own mind—Stub Alison, Big Leaguer. He glanced at the craggy-faced, thick-shouldered man who was walking slowly toward the third-base coaching box.

Country Selder, five years a Goliath coach but still remembered by fans as a great hitter and left fielder, eyed the rookie. Fans knew from sports-sheet writing that Country Selder was responsible for Alison being jumped from high-school diamonds to the big league. The same fog-horn voice resounded from the stands.

"So this hammered-down character is your boy, Selder! That the way you coached him to play left field? If he looks like a big leaguer to you, you need your eyes examined!"

Country Selder gave no evidence that he heard the derisive yell. "Tough wind currents out there today, kid." He spoke easily in his soft Georgia drawl. "Downdraft between the upper deck and bleachers. Shadows this time of year make it rough to pick up a drive right off, too. Hang in there, kid, you hear?"

"Yeah."

Stub glanced at the grizzled coach. He looked quickly down again and did not slow his pace. Country Selder wasn't fooling anybody. Selder knew that line drive had been misjudged from here to Kalamazoo. Stub swallowed dryly and did not look at Selder as he muttered again, "Yeah!"

He was as fully aware as any of the fans that the 3 to 1

lead on the scoreboard for the visiting Hoppers was up there solely because of his inept outfield play. Country Selder knew it. Manager Mule Sully knew it. The drive had not been a really tough chance.

Stub Alison, Big Leaguer—what a laugh! Any other outfielder in the league—any *outfielder* in *any* league— would have gloved the drive without difficulty. It would have been the third out of the inning. Three big, unearned runs would never have gone on the board for the Hoppers.

"So they stick a fellow in a spot he never played before!" Stub muttered to himself a moment before he reached the Goliath dugout. "What can they expect? I never claimed to be anything but a catcher!"

If the rookie had any faint idea that once he reached the dugout, he reached sanctuary, he was sorely and quickly disillusioned.

"Some rookies come up to the big time with at least a little on the ball." The rasping voice of Ark Molton filled the dugout. The big Goliath first baseman and power slugger flicked a glance down the bench and added: "Then, again, some bushers come up figuring they can just *talk* a good game. We sure drew a talker, huh?"

"Yeah!"

It was more a grunt than a word from big Mike Clancy. The veteran right fielder spat.

"Could be some of us worn-out cripples ought to have crutches." Clancy sneered and glared at Stub. "But I'll give any odds you want that none of us would rare in for a line drive like it was an easy flyball—and watch it sail past to the barrier!"

Stub's ears were still red from the scathing remarks fans

had hurled his way. Now they deepened a darker crimson. He knew that the not-so-subtle ridicule was aimed at him, but there wasn't much he could do about it.

I've got a blistering coming, he thought. No use trying to explain that Kendrick sold me a bill of goods. I shot plenty of barbs into those guys. I can't kick because they're handing them back. The thing was, there was that vicious undertone of sour dislike in the veterans' needling. That got a fellow down.

Stub glanced the length of the dugout toward a long-legged, darkly handsome player who slouched on the bench near the water fountain. Duke Kendrick met his gaze for a moment, frowning slightly. He shrugged then and his eyes slid away from Stub's gaze.

That gag the Duke sold me sure was a bill of goods, Stub thought. The rookie's gaze encountered other players on the bench: Ted Fox, in his eighth year as Goliath shortstop, still cat-quick and smart; Henry Schmidt, veteran third baseman, huge and slow of speech and almost as slow of foot; Roger Samron, young and fleet, a very good ballplayer now, starting his third season in center field. Samron showed a bright potential for real greatness. Monk Banyan, second baseman. Jim Hayes, the man whose place Stub Alison had taken today; Jake Dahl and Tony De-Mino, veteran mainstays of the Goliath catching staff; were looking at him with no expression at all. Rog Samron gave his head a little shake as though commiserating with a fellow sufferer of the freak wind currents and shadows of Goliath Stadium. Samron's eyes were friendly. All the others were hard and they were grim of visage.

A hurt bewilderment came into the rookie's blue eyes. He took off the yellow-visored cap with the black G on the front. He ran a hand through crew-cut hair that was the color of the red clay found in his native Georgia.

Doggone it, wouldn't these hard-shelled guys ever relax? Couldn't they let down the bars just a teeny bit? It was for sure they would be met more than halfway.

Again Stub threw a glance toward Duke Kendrick. Funny that he felt no animosity toward Kendrick, but then there hadn't been any law requiring him to buy the dark-haired southpaw's gag that first day he'd reported to the Goliaths.

He counted mentally. This was the tenth day that Stub Alison had worn a Goliath uniform. He'd been so sure that everything would straighten out when—and if—Manager Mule Sully gave him a chance to play. Country Selder had assured him from the start that he'd get a chance to show his stuff. That the chance would be playing left field never entered his thoughts.

He should have suspected something when Country Selder had him report every morning at the stadium. He should have known that Selder would not have been handing out tips about playing balls that caromed off the barrier, judging angles, learning wind currents. Selder wouldn't have hit a catcher nine hundred fungoes and run a fellow's legs off fielding them. He wouldn't have cautioned a catcher about such things as heeding the crunch of spikes on the warning track when going top speed after a drive.

Stub Alison had never played outfield. Stub Alison was

a catcher. But he knew deep down that being shoved into an outfield spot for his debut was only part of the sour business. Mostly it went back to that first day. If only Molton and Clancy and Banyan and Fox and the other veterans would forget that day.

"—one thing about it." Stub became abruptly aware that Monk Banyan's loud words were strictly for him. The squat second baseman went on: "There's no real cause for alarm because the Hoppers were handed three gift runs. All it takes is for a couple of us creaky-jointed, ready-for-the-scrap-heap gents to get on base. The mouthy busher is due at the dish this inning. He's a cinch to *talk* the Hopper chucker out of at least an extra base knock!"

Despair filled Stub for a moment. He stared at the toes of his spikes, emotions hanging as low as his head. He wondered briefly if things would have been any different if Manager Mule Sully hadn't been bounced by the umpire in the first inning.

Suddenly the natural battling instinct that went with his hair and square, rugged chin asserted itself in Stub. A flaming resolution was born in the stocky rookie. He never knew whether he muttered aloud or strictly for his own mental hearing.

"Okay, so maybe I'll never be a big leaguer. I fell for Kendrick's gag and these tough monkeys aren't willing to overlook it. If they want war, I'll show them Stub Alison is a big leaguer in the needling department, anyway!"

CHAPTER TWO

A Coach and a Sports Writer Wonder

Country Selder stood in the third-base coaching box. He twitched at his cap visor. He passed his right hand across the letters on his shirt front. He smoothed the letters with his left hand. He hitched at his belt. He rubbed a hand across the back of his neck and wiped the same hand on the shoulder of his flannel shirt.

He went through more motions. Only one motion of all those he made meant anything. Touching cloth immediately after touching flesh with either hand was the current Goliath "hit" sign. Touching flesh immediately after cloth would have been the "take" sign. All the other motions were merely thrown in to confuse sign stealers of the rival ball club.

"Be alive up there, Monk!" Selder clapped his hands together as he called to the batter. "Make him come in there with that apple. Make it be good!"

Monk Banyan tapped his bat once on the plate. That was an answer to the hit sign Country Selder had passed.

Selder knew that Mule Sully would probably not have given Banyan the green light on the first pitch. Country Selder sometimes wondered if Sully didn't overmanage. Was it necessary to signal from the bench for veteran hitters like Monk Banyan to hit or take? Mule Sully insisted on such procedure, but Mule Sully had been banished from the dugout for arguing an umpire's decision in the top of the first inning. Country Selder was giving the managerial orders the rest of this ball game.

Monk Banyan tied into a fast ball pitched to the high outside corner. He hit the ball "where it was pitched." A low liner sizzled through the hole between first and second basemen.

"The way to go, way to go-o-o!" Again Selder clapped his hands. He paced up and down the coaching box making motions. About in the middle of them he passed the hit-and-run sign to Tony DeMino. The veteran catcher acknowledged the signal.

The Goliaths played the hit-and-run more often than a sacrifice, especially in the early innings. The Goliath batting order had hitting power almost anywhere down to the pitcher. Tony DeMino made his own sign to Monk Banyan. It was to be on the first pitch. Banyan was under way with the pitcher's delivery motion.

DeMino slashed a ground hit through the area vacated by the shortstop who ran to cover second. Monk Banyan kept right on going. The Hopper outfielder who fielded the hit thought there was a chance to throw Banyan out and heaved a peg to third. The play was close but Banyan earned the umpire's decision. Tony DeMino, huge and slow, nevertheless lumbered safely down to second on the play.

Runners on third and second. Nobody out. Hopper defensive strategy might be to fill up the extra base and play for a double play, conceding the Goliaths one run. Also the Hopper manager might order his pitcher to work on the next batter and then fill the empty base if they could get him out.

Stub Alison was due at the plate. Here was a rookie that Hopper pitchers had never had opportunity to work on. And Country Selder had already violated the book. Would he cross the Hoppers again, have the youngster pull something fancy like a squeeze bunt?

Country Selder paced the coaching box, making signals and signal-hiding motions like crazy. His back was to the plate when the base umpire spoke in a low tone.

"The kid called time, Country." The umpire inclined his head toward Stub Alison, walking toward the coaching box. "Guess he wants to make sure he got the sign."

It was not the sign that bothered Stub. He carried a bat but his blue eyes held a question. It had occurred to him that Country Selder was out on a limb. If Mule Sully had been in the Goliath dugout, Stub Alison would probably have been yanked after that fiasco in the field. Country Selder came to meet Stub.

"I thought maybe you'd want to get off the hook and send a pinch hitter up there for me," Stub said.

Country Selder eyed the rookie steadily. He answered

softly, "You want to hit, kid, or have you lost your nerve!"

Stub flushed. He clenched his jaw and spoke through set teeth. "I haven't lost my nerve! I want to hit!"

"Then get up there and rap one! They'll figure we're setting something up. Take the first two. After that, clobber the first pitch that's near enough to nail!"

Stub did not know that a moment after he turned back toward the plate Country Selder cursed himself silently. Sending a green kid up there at the dish for his first major-league at bat, with instructions you'd give a seasoned veteran!

The youngster felt different at the plate than he had in left field. He loved to hit. The Hopper battery proved to have figured as Selder surmised. The first pitch was a sweeping curve, high and away outside. The next was a high, fast ball, close in on Stub's fists. He gripped his bat a little more tightly. The next one would be in the strike zone or very near it.

The pitch was a fast ball down the inside edge just a little below the letters. Stub's bat flashed around in smooth, level swing at the grayish-white streak.

Crack!

He caught the fireball on the good wood of his bat. A clothesline drive whistled over the second baseman's leap. The drive hit the turf between the outfielders. Stub raced around first. He cut the inside corner of the bag at second. Country Selder urged him to come on with a pulling, waving motion.

The throw from the outfielder to the shortstop and the relay to third were perfect. Stub slid, twisted his body away from the bag, but the ball was on him before he hooked the bag.

"Okay, kid, okay!" Country Selder helped Stub brush off his uniform. "That was a real poke! You had a legitimate try for three and don't let anybody tell you different!"

Stub nodded. He did not relish being thrown out, but Hopper fielders were major leaguers, too. You expected sharp play from major leaguers.

Nothing could take away the satisfaction of that solid base hit. Two runs batted in were not to be sneezed at by any hitter. He felt much better as he trotted toward the dugout. He really expected a little thaw in the atmosphere.

Instead, a heavy silence greeted him. It seemed as though the old-timers resented the fact that he'd come through and shut off opportunity for them to gripe. Stub swallowed a lump that came abruptly into his throat. He slumped dejectedly to the bench.

What was the use? You'd think they might give one grunt of approval or something to hearten a fellow a little. No, they were never going to forgive that first day.

Stub sat hunched on the bench and recalled events of the day he reported to the Goliaths.

It was a Monday and an off day in the schedule. But the Goliaths had just finished a disastrous road trip, lost a series to the last-place Hillies to climax it. Mule Sully ordered a workout for the day off. Country Selder, the man who had signed Stub Alison and the youngster's hero for years, was not in the clubhouse when Stub reported. The coach had left word with the clubhouse attendant to outfit the rookie.

Stub learned afterward that, as far as Manager Sully was concerned, he became a Goliath with two strikes on him before he ever swung a bat or threw a ball. Sully liked big, powerful men on his club.

The stocky rookie was not a midget by ordinary standards. Still his five-seven and one sixty-five pounds stacked up small beside the six-four and six-three and two hundred pounds plus of Ark Molton and Mike Clancy. Other veterans were in the same general size class.

"Ma-a-an, they're *really* Goliaths!" Stub made the observation aloud. "A fellow better sing kind of small 'round guys that big, I bet!"

"There's where you're wrong." A tall but slender player who had dark hair grinned at Stub as the rookie whirled around. "Name's Kendrick," the tall player said. "Pitcher. I just came up myself last year. Confidentially, I learned the hard way that there's only one way to get along with these big bozos. Whittle 'em down to size. Let 'em know from the start that you take no guff!"

"Hey!" Stub grinned good-naturedly. "I'm a cracker from the Georgia hill country, all right," he said, "but after all!"

"I'm telling you right." Kendrick shrugged. "Go ahead and learn the rough way, it's no skin off me."

"Wouldn't it be pretty cocky for me to sass big stars like these fellows?"

"The cockier you are, the better. Did you ever hear of Dizzy Dean? He came up to the big time from backwoods Arkansas, or some place down there. *He* told 'em—and they liked it!"

Duke Kendrick filled the rookie to the chin. Stub never quite lost a deep-seated doubt. But he more than halfway bought the bill of goods that the slender pitcher peddled.

Mostly because Molton and Clancy and the rest fired shafts at me first, Stub thought there in the dugout. He recalled Ark Molton's attitude that first day.

"Well, well," the big first baseman said as he winked at Mike Clancy, "looks like the front office finally loosened up and sent us a bat boy. Run back to the clubhouse and fetch my eatin' tobacco, sonny!"

That was the moment when Stub began to think that Duke Kendrick had given him a straight steer. He looked Ark Molton up and down then grinned. He let the hulking first-base veteran have both barrels.

"I'm not the bat boy," Stub said in his soft Georgia drawl. "I'm the fellow the front office sent out to inject a little life into this gang of Charley-horsed antiques!"

Stub pointedly eyed the bulging roll around Molton's middle.

"Seems as though it would be a better idea for *you* to run back to the clubhouse—and on around the field twenty times! Maybe you could reduce that German goitre so it doesn't look like a spare tire! I'm not a bat boy, I'm a ballplayer!"

Ark Molton nearly had apoplexy. Stub could not have known that Mule Sully had jumped Molton only the day before about being so badly overweight.

"A wisenheimer, yet!" Ark Molton snorted. "So you're a ballplayer. I suppose you play first base—for a Little League team!"

"I'm a catcher! And I can hold up my end with—"

"What goes on here?"

Manager Sully had come across the diamond. He scowled as he sized up Stub, then grunted. "Selder didn't say anything about you being a catcher," the manager said. "We're supposed to have bought a bat when we signed you. This is no softball league. A major-league backstop needs plenty of beef to absorb the shock of fast-ball pitching for nine innings."

"I can take all the stuff any pitcher on this club has, softball or not!"

Stub would never forget the black scowl that suddenly twisted the heavy features of Mule Sully.

"Another would-be manager, huh!" Sully snorted, "besides being an already-developed big-league catcher. Get this, rookie: until the front office says otherwise, I'm running this ball club!"

It hadn't seemed reasonable to Stub that the manager should have flared such anger, but from that moment he felt that he was in Sully's doghouse. He knew without question that he did not click with veteran members of the Goliaths.

Clancy, Molton, Fox, Banyan—all of them, on occasion —gave him an unmerciful riding. Still, Stub Alison owned a stubborn streak. He refused to take the abuse lying down. He rode them back, and sometimes the veterans found themselves badly outneedled.

Country Selder gave the rookie the word that Duke Kendrick was an inveterate joker and that the southpaw had pulled off a large gag, but the daily word war between Stub Alison and the veterans did not ease.

Stub suddenly sat straighter there in the dugout. Why, there was the whole thing. It was truly a kind of war. Was he going to let Molton and his cronies drive him into quitting? Well! He'd show these crusty veterans.

The Goliaths took a two-run lead that inning. Lefty Byrnes drew a fat salary check from the Goliaths for firing southpaw slants that enemy batters could not handle well, but Byrnes was a better-than-fair hitting pitcher. He singled after Stub was thrown out.

The Hoppers brought a relief pitcher in from the bull-pen. Fox greeted the Hopper fireman by dumping a base hit over the infield. Rog Samron beat a sinker into the dirt down the first-base line. He was nipped at first base but the effect was the same as if he had laid down a sacrifice bunt. DeMino stood on third and Fox on second. Two runs in position to score on a hit.

Henry Schmidt supplied the base hit, a clean smash to left center.

The Goliath lead held up till the sixth inning. In the top of that frame Stub Alison badly misplayed a hit that caromed off the barrier. A runner scored from first base and the hitter reached third. Then Stub caught a routine fly, medium deep—and heaved the ball into the Goliath dugout in an attempted peg home.

He knocked in another run in the Goliath seventh and scored himself by fine, heads-up base running. Then disaster overtook him again in the eighth.

The Hoppers got three men on base and two out. Lefty tightened in the clutch. He induced a left-handed batter to go after a wide pitch. He sliced a looping fly to left field, an easy chance.

Stub Alison lost the ball in the late-afternoon shadows from the stands. He didn't come within three feet of catching the fly.

Still, figures on the scoreboard at the end of the game showed Goliaths, 9; Hoppers, 8. Stub Alison had accounted for four Goliath runs with a potent bat, but his inept fielding was mainly responsible for all of the Hopper scores.

"Can a rookie who gives away twice as many runs as he accounts for stay in the big league?"

Milton Binkley, *Gazette* sports writer who had covered Goliath games more than twenty years, was asked the question up in the press box. Binkley was a slender man of medium height who was never seen without a battered gray hat atop his head. Curious people who asked why he always wore the hat were informed that it was because he had no hair. They invariably accepted that as kidding.

The fact was that the only hair Binkley had was the sparse fringe that showed above his ears and across the back of his neck. He pushed the hat a little higher and eyed the questioner.

"That's a blamed good question," Binkley said. "I wouldn't even guess at answering it. I'll wander down to the clubhouse, though, and see whether a better qualified man than yours truly can come up with the answer."

He found Country Selder slouched in a scarred chair before the desk in the small clubhouse office used by

Goliath managers. Selder sat staring at the wall and frowning. He looked up.

"Well, well, and well!" Binkley's gray eyes gleamed. "Don't tell me the front office finally wised up and ousted Sully and put you in the job! I'm not going to ask what's with Sully. Arguing with an umpire over a called strike and blowing up and getting bounced clear out of the park! For my money the guy needs a psychiatrist. I honestly believe the man's sick. The club sure would be better off if they made you permanent man—"

"Hold it, Bink!" Country Selder interrupted. "I came in here because I thought Sully would be here. He just phoned that he wouldn't be. Frankly, Bink, I'm in no mood to give out good copy. Make it fast, will you? I'd like to catch Alison before he leaves the stadium."

"Okay, Country." Binkley shrugged. "Here it is: how about the Alison kid? He got two for four and both were solid drives. That Hopper right fielder nabbed one off him that would have been long gone if the kid had pulled it four feet more. Alison looks like a hitter, for sure, but can he keep a bat somewhere approaching that hot after the pitchers get a good look at him?"

"Nobody can guarantee that big-league pitchers won't root out weakness in any batter." Country Selder spoke in the soft drawl that even twenty years of being away from his Georgia home most of the time had not changed. "The kid is a natural hitter. He's got a good eye and his swing is smooth and level and sweet. He gets a terrific whip snap. I've checked on him in off-season play down in our country. I wouldn't have recommended that the club sign him if I didn't believe wholeheartedly that Alison has the equipment to develop into a good, dependable hitter. Maybe even a great hitter!"

Binkley waited a little space of time for Selder to continue. The coach was apparently through speaking.

"That all you care to put out on the rookie?" Binkley finally asked.

"For the record, yes." Country Selder nodded then eyed the sports writer. They had been friends since Selder broke in with the Goliaths the same season that Binkley started covering the club. The coach sighed. "Off the record," he said, "I'm wondering about the kid as much as you."

"Always ask a gent who knows when you want the straight scoop." A wry grin wrinkled Binkley's face. "I know almost as much now as when I came down."

The sports writer eyed Country Selder. "Are you wondering whether he can knock in enough runs to overbalance the ones his fielding will let in? And it's outright generosity to call what Alison did today fielding!"

"Something like that, Bink, but not exactly." Again Country Selder sighed. "I can teach the kid to play outfield, if he wants to learn. The trouble is, Stub Alison wants to be a catcher. He can catch, too. What I'm wondering is whether I can convince him there's more future in playing the outfield before Mule Sully ships him deep down in the sticks!"

CHAPTER THREE

Down to a Class D Farm Club

Manager Mule Sully received a telegram an hour before the second game of the Hopper Series. The wire was from the office of the league president. The Goliath public-relations man released copies of the wire to sports writers.

> CAREFUL CONSIDERATION OF FACTS IN UMPIRE REPORT
> YESTERDAY DISGRACEFUL INCIDENT REQUIRES DECISION
> THIS OFFICE THAT YOU BE SUSPENDED THREE PLAYING
> DAYS. FINE OF TWO HUNDRED FIFTY DOLLARS MUST BE
> RECEIVED THIS OFFICE BEFORE REINSTATEMENT.

"He had it coming." Binkley pushed the rim of his hat up a bit. "Just like I said yesterday, Sully needs a psychiatrist. He's always been a bullhead, but lately he acts like a gent gone completely off his rocker!"

"You know, Bink, I'm about ready to buy that." The remark came in thoughtful tone from a rotund sports writer of another paper. "I've gone along with Sully, but everybody knows the league rule that a manager or coach draws an automatic fine if he starts a rhubarb with an umpire unless a rule interpretation is involved. From what I hear, Sully passed out some real mule-skinner language to the umps. That's probably why the suspension and stiff fine."

"There's one good thing about it," Binkley said. "Country Selder will manage the club while Sully is in the pokey. The Goliaths'll have consistent direction for a change. They might even come up with a streak of more than one consecutive win!"

Country Selder gave Stub Alison a brief talk before the game.

"Forget that ball game yesterday, kid," Selder said. "You're out there in left again. You're batting back of Banyan. Try to remember the things I told you about playing the wall rebounds and allowing for wind currents and shadows, you hear?"

The youngster nodded. He was grateful to Country Selder. Being moved up a notch in the batting order was all right. And hearing that "you hear" tacked on made a fellow feel more at home. That was pure deep South, for sure.

Pete Ryder, burly right-hander, had his stuff that day. He had the Hoppers shut out on a measly three hits going into the bottom of the eighth, but a young bonus pitcher, fresh out of college, worked for the Hoppers, and he gave every evidence that he was worth the bonus paid him to sign a Hopper contract. The collegian had allowed the murderous batting order of the Goliaths a meager five hits, all singles and well scattered. No base runner had got farther than second for either team.

Stub Alison lined to the second baseman his first time at bat. He chased the right fielder to the barrier to grab a well-hit drive the second time he went to the plate. He led off the seventh with a clean hit to right center. Then the rookie was erased in a double play that should have been no more than a force-out on him.

Monk Banyan rapped the ball sharply to deep short. It was fielded cleanly and the Hoppers naturally went for the double play. Stub yelled and flung himself in a wild slide that was half block. Whether the yell had anything to do with it or not, the Hopper second baseman juggled the ball in leaping clear.

There was no question that Stub was forced out. But the relay to first was weak and should have been too late to double Banyan. The Goliath veteran was guilty of slowing when the shortstop fielded the ball.

He put on a belated burst of speed when the second baseman juggled the throw. Too late. Even the weak throw beat Banyan by a hair.

"You can't talk a guy out of making the twin killing, busher!" Banyan snarled at Stub as they entered the dugout. "Didn't anybody ever tell you to barrel in there and take the pivot man out?"

"Yeah," Ark Molton chipped in. "You're such a cute, fresh rookie—but you don't have the guts to make a real tough play!"

Stub stared unbelievingly for a second. Banyan just

couldn't be trying to sneak off the hook of his own inexcusable sloppy base running! But he was. And Molton hammered on the needling theme to help out a veteran pal.

"Who do you fellows think you're kidding?" Stub drawled the question. "I *did* barrel into the pivot man. And that or something made him juggle the throw from short. If your spavined old joints can't carry you down to first base without a twenty-minute stop for rest, it's time something was done about it!"

Molton and Banyan glared. Banyan muttered something that the rookie did not hear. Molton growled, "You're going to lip off too much, rookie!"

Country Selder met Banyan at the dugout when DeMino ended the inning by flying to left.

"You want me to send a replacement out there for you, Banyan?" Selder asked.

"Replacement?" Banyan looked quickly at the acting manager. "What do you mean?"

"Why, I thought you must have pulled a muscle or strained a ligament or something." Selder's tone was soft. Suddenly it hardened. "That crummy base running cost you fifty bucks," he said. "Any more lousy rocks that stem from pure laziness will cost a hundred. That goes for everybody, you hear!"

Stub Alison lost a flyball that inning. Pete Ryder pitched over the error, but Monk Banyan grumbled in the dugout when Country Selder was out of earshot.

"I get handed a fifty-dollar fine for nothing, but a mouthy rookie gets away with bush-league fielding for free!"

The young Hopper pitcher retired the first two batters in the Goliath eighth. Then his control deserted him momentarily. He walked Pete Fox. Samron refused to go after tempting pitches and also drew free transportation to first. A sharp breaking curve nicked Schmidt's shirt front and the bases were loaded for big Mike Clancy. Clancy slammed a drive through the box that looked labeled base hit.

The Hopper second baseman managed to reach it. His hard, accurate throw beat Clancy to the bag by half a step. The drive would have been a hit for a faster man.

Pete Ryder set the Hoppers down one, two, three in the top of the ninth.

"Let's get on this college boy," somebody said in the Goliath dugout. "And go home. They don't pay us extra dough for overtime!"

"It won't go into extra innings." Mike Clancy spoke loudly. "Look at the batting order. Molton, Banyan, and Alison. *Alison!* The hot-shot rook will see that we don't work overtime!"

"If some of you worn-out, used-to-be hot shots could get off the nickel, we'd be taking showers right now," Stub drawled. "Oil up those creaky old joints and move fast enough to get on base and we just might score a run!"

Mike Clancy muttered under his breath. Ark Molton glowered at the youngster. The big slugger mumbled to himself as he went to bat. He nearly ended the game on the first pitch. Only a spectacular, leaping grab by a Hopper outfielder snared the ball a second's fraction before it would have cleared the left-field barrier.

Monk Banyan drove the same fielder to deep left center to drag down his drive. Stub Alison went to the plate.

"There's only two out, kid! Hang in there and bust one!"

Country Selder called encouragement from third-base coaching box. He passed Stub the take sign. The rookie looked over the first pitch. It was a breaking ball that missed the strike zone.

"Hang in there and bust one, kid!" Selder yelled again. He passed the hit sign while he yelled.

Stub hung in there and "busted" one. He timed a sinking curve perfectly, lashed a wicked ground hit through the box. The ball caromed off second base past a charging shortstop into short left field. Stub turned on all the speed he owned. He went into second with a stand-up double. He stood on the bag and yelled toward the plate as DeMino took his stance.

"All right, all right! Oil things up and let's go!"

DeMino hadn't handed the rookie as many barbs as Clancy and Molton and Banyan although he had thrown in his two cents' worth a couple of times. He looked nettled enough to maybe "oil things up." But the Hopper bench ordered DeMino walked.

Country Selder expected the strategy. Fill up an empty base and make a force play possible at third and second, and bring Pete Ryder to bat. Pete Ryder, who held a paid-up card in the Pitchers Aren't-Paid-to-Hit-And-don't Association. Country Selder countered the Hopper strategy by sending Jake Dahl up there to pinch hit for Ryder.

"Don't put the oil can away!" Stub again yelled from second base. "We still need a bingle!"

Jake Dahl was in the same category as DeMino. He hadn't been really active in the needlework but he had let Stub know that he strung along with Molton and Company. Now he moved in the batter's box as though Stub's crack got under his skin.

Dahl blasted the third pitch between right and center fielders. It would have been a two-base hit, but as quickly as Stub's spikes bit the rubber of home plate, the game was over. Dahl made sure that he touched the bag at first and ran for the clubhouse.

In the final game of the series next day, the Goliaths outlasted the Hoppers 9 to 7 in another high-scoring game. A series sweep. Stub Alison went one for four, his hit being a solid smash with the bases loaded which drove in two runs, but he goofed twice in outfield play. One error of omission cost two Hopper runs.

"Well, the kid broke even today and I'd say a little more than even yesterday." Binkley made the observation in the press box. "Maybe a puff in my column will give our young Mr. Alison a lift."

Binkley headed his piece for the *Gazette* SULLY-LESS GOLIATHS SWEEP SERIES.

It was a rather biting criticism of Mule Sully, in a left-hand fashion. In passing, the sports writer gave part credit for the sweep to Stub Alison. The paragraph that did the damage to Stub Alison—and later to Country Selder—closed Binkley's column:

"*. . . It is the first sweep of a series the erstwhile slipping veterans have notched since the first week of the season. Could Sully's Slipping Sluggers have finally begun to click? This corner holds that two things are responsible. One: consistency in managerial tactics from Country Selder the past three days showed in game results. Two: the potent bat wielded by Rookie Stub Alison—five hits in eleven at bats for a gaudy .454 average and six runs batted in! Could also be that needling the rookie and vets engage in keeps the whole club a bit more alive.*"

The Goliaths won the opening game of the Savage series. Stub Alison hit two for five, drove in a pair of runs, and scored one himself—and messed up a drive that caromed off the barrier in left that allowed a Savage unearned run.

He experienced no especial qualms when the clubhouse attendant informed him before the second Savage game that he was to report to the manager's office. Mule Sully was seated behind the desk. His suspension had been served and his fine paid. Sully did not beat around the bush.

"You're not suiting out today, Alison," Sully said. "You're going down to the Goliath Dees. Pick up your plane ticket at the front office. The Dees expect you in time to suit out for them tonight!"

Stub stared, stunned speechless. His jaw hung slack. He hadn't really expected to stick with the parent big-league club right from high school. He had been prepared to spend time in the farm system. Maybe a year or two with a Triple A club or at the least with a Double A club.

Shipped to the Dees! The Dees were in a Class D league, the lowest classification league! The Dees were in last place in their Class D league!

Mule Sully looked up at the open-mouthed youngster. A black scowl abruptly wrinkled Sully's heavy face.

"It shouldn't be such a shock," Sully said. "You should know that you'd have been down there from the start except that Selder sold me a— Well, never mind that. Maybe Selder and his wise sports-writer stooge are due to learn Mule Sully can't be pushed around, too!"

CHAPTER FOUR

Surprises

The first surprise came when Stub asked a question of the man who weighed his baggage and checked his tickets at the airport.

"What sort of place is this I'm going to?" Stub asked. "A backwoods hamlet, or something?"

"Oh, no! It isn't New York or Chicago, of course, or even anywhere near as big as this place, but you'll find a pleasant, small city."

"Will this flight take me directly there?"

"Well, no." The airport man smiled. "I didn't mean to infer that it's important enough to warrant the larger flights. Still, you'll make only one change of planes. The shuttle line to that city adapts their flights very nicely to ours. I'm sure there will be little or no waitover."

The next surprise came when Stub stepped off the plane after the second leg of his journey. The airport was not a

LaGuardia Field or a Miami International Airport or a Willow Run. Neither was it any small-town setup. He climbed into the taxi at the head of a line of eight or ten cabs outside the busy airport terminal. He asked to be taken to the hotel.

"The hotel?" The cabdriver raised his brows. "Am I supposed to know which hotel you mean? We're not exactly a hick crossroad village with just one hotel, Mac!"

Stub felt the blood flush up his neck. He should have known from the way that fellow at the airport had talked, and the bustling activity around him, that this city would support more than one hotel. He was acting like a country boy.

Well, I *am* a country boy, he thought. He grinned at the cabdriver. "I didn't mean to make out your town is a hick crossroad village," he said. "It's more me being the hick. Take me to a hotel that's near the ball park and doesn't charge awfully high rates. Ballplayers on a Class D salary can't afford ritzy hotels, that's for sure."

The cabdriver peered sharply at Stub. "Okay, Mac," he said. "No harm done. You a ballplayer, Mac?"

"Well, that's a question." Stub's grin was a little wry. "I think so, but Mister Sully doesn't go along with my opinion!"

"Mister Sully? Mule Sully, manager of the big-time Goliaths? You been playing with the Goliaths, Mac? I'm a baseball buff. If you're good enough to have been up there with the big boys, believe me you'll be welcome here! The Dees can sure use some ballplayers. What's your name, Mac?"

Stub told him. Again the taxi man peered sharply at the youngster.

"Are you the Alison who had a hitting streak hot as a prairie fire and racked up umpteen runs-batted-in and played left field for the Goliaths?"

"There's another question." Again Stub's grin was on the wry side. "I was lucky enough to get a few hits and my share of RBI's. I have to admit to being out there in left field, too, but whether I *played* left field—well, Mister Sully didn't think so!"

Stub Alison sighed. "I tried to tell him I'm a catcher," he said. "Maybe the Dees will give a fellow a chance to play a spot he knows something about playing! Doggone it, I listened to Country Selder and signed a Goliath contract mostly because I thought I'd have more chance to break in with a club that carries an aging catching staff. Man, was I ever wrong! Looks as though Mister Sully counts on DeMino and Dahl going on forever!"

"Outfield or catcher, Mac, it's a cinch you'll get plenty of action with the Dees. You'll be in there tonight, huh?"

Stub nodded. Sully had told him the Dees expected him to suit out for their game tonight.

He registered at the hotel and learned that the ball park was only ten blocks away. He ate a light meal, lounged in a chair in the hotel lobby, and read the sports sheet of the local paper. The Dees had absorbed a real clobbering the night before, 12 to 2. The final paragraph in the account of the game interested Stub:

"... *Your correspondent has been informed by Dees officials that playing help is being sent from the*

*Goliath chain. Rumor around the ball yard has it
that besides new playing help, a change in the master-
minding department is imminent. We have no quarrel
with the current Dees manager. However, a thorough
renovating might be the tonic our ball club needs.
Dees fans are becoming a little weary of a last, LAST,*
last *place club!"*

Stub reported to the ball park two hours before game
time. It was a surprisingly nice park for Class D. The
grandstand and bleachers would probably accommodate
ten thousand fans and were steel and concrete. The infield
was well kept. The outfield was cleanly mowed and looked
smooth. Stub understood why things were so professional
when he read words below the scoreboard in right field.

DEES FIELD

WINTER HOME OF
GOLIATH MINOR-LEAGUE CLUBS

Stub found a door beneath the stands marked *Dees
Dressing Room.* The door was locked. Stub prowled
farther. Somebody must be around. He finally spied a slender figure coming from a door at the other end of the
grandstand. It was lettered *Visiting Team Dressing Room.*

The slender man wore a blue baseball cap with a bright
orange D above the visor. He saw Stub and frowned.

"Must have left the blasted gate unhooked," he muttered. Then to Stub: "You'll have to wait till the ticket
window opens, young fellow. Must be a real fan, getting
out here this early. The players won't even show up for
another half-hour."

"I'm not a fan," Stub said. "I'm a ballplayer." He grinned as the words recalled the taxi man's reaction. "Maybe I'd better say I'm supposed to be a ballplayer. I had orders from Mister Sully to report to the Dees in time to suit out for tonight's game. I'm Alison. Can you tell me where I'll find the manager?"

"Alison, Alison." The man who wore the blue baseball cap lifted it and frowned a little as he repeated Stub's name. Then abruptly his face cleared. "Sure, you're the youngster the Goliaths signed right out of high school!"

The man stuck out his hand. "Name of Monahan. Coach, trainer, equipment manager, just about you-name-it-and-I-do-it for the ball club. I can't tell you where to find the manager, though. He phoned me couple of hours ago and said I'd be in charge tonight. Hung up before I could ask any questions."

"Then it looks as though I report to you," Stub said. "Where do I get a suit?"

"Hold on a minute, now! I don't know as you can report to me— Well, sure, you can report. What I mean is, I haven't been able to locate the business manager. Nobody has said anything to me about you coming in. I could give you a suit but I wouldn't dare stick you in the lineup till I had some authority from the brass."

Monahan looked at Stub. "You might as well give yourself a busman's holiday and watch a ball game, Alison." The leathery face of the Dees' all-purpose man wrinkled in a rueful grin. "That is, if the kind of performance this gang likely will put out can be called a ball game. The trouble is, Alison, there are wheels within wheels, like they say. Something's going on with the ball club that I don't know about. I'm not going to stick my neck out if I can help it."

Stub Alison sat high in the stands behind home plate. Just for fun, the youngster pretended that he was catching for the Dees. As each batter of the visiting club came to the plate, Stub sized him up. He studied the batter's stance. Did he stand close to the plate or back? Was he deep in the batter's box, medium, or up front? Then Stub decided mentally what pitch he would sign for and where he would hold his mitt for a target.

Stub's call and the pitch rarely agreed. There was no way for him to tell whether it was lack of control on the part of the pitchers when the pitch came in high when he had decided it should be low, or vice versa, but he could tell a little from the catcher's mitt target. Also, he knew when the pitch was a curve or fast ball or slider or change-up.

He was bothered at first because his calls and the Dees' catcher's call did not coincide. Soon he was not bothered. Rival batters were murdering the Dees' pitching.

The third hurler was on the mound for the Dees in the seventh inning. Hitters of the other club had slammed the Dees' pitching to all corners of the ball park. They had notched fifteen base hits, nine of them for extra bases.

It's most likely just plain, ineffective pitching, Stub thought, but it could be wrong kinds of pitches called for by the catcher. Just maybe a fellow could get a chance to work behind the bat down here!

His pulse quickened at the thought. If things turned out that way, being sent down from the Goliaths might turn out to be a good break.

The Dees took another bad licking that night, 11 to 5.

Stub went down to the dressing room. It was in his mind to learn if Monahan had heard anything, or if the business manager had returned. Stub ran into the biggest of all surprises this surprising day had produced.

Country Selder was standing beside Monahan before an open locker. Stub heard Selder say, "I'll keep the same locker, Pat. Looks as though the uniform hanging there will fit."

A smile creased the leathery face of Pat Monahan. "I'm right glad you'll keep it," he said. "Mine's right here beside it. Kind of like that season we had lockers side by side in the old Three I league. Remember, Country?"

"I remember. The Goliaths called me up at the end of the season and you went up for a trial with the Bucks." Selder nodded. "There have been a lot of baseballs heaved wild since then, Pat."

Selder turned and saw Alison, and his craggy face wrinkled in a half-grin. "Surprise, kid," he drawled. "Looks like you and me are stuck with each other again. The Goliaths shipped me down here to take over as manager!"

CHAPTER FIVE

Maybe Better Off

Country Selder had chalked a notice on the square of blackened wallboard near the door in the Dees' dressing quarters. It called for the players to report two hours before game time the next night. Next day the new Dees manager phoned Stub in midafternoon and arranged for the rookie to eat with him.

"I know you wouldn't get any idea about being favored," Selder said when he met Stub. "I don't want any of the other boys to get such an idea, either. Away from the ball park is one thing. Out there, you're the same as any other player, you hear?"

"I hear." Stub chuckled. "Fine way to bark at a fellow from your home county, I'd say! Seriously, you ought to know I wouldn't want it any other way."

"Good," Selder nodded, "but there are a couple of things we need to talk about privately. First off, like Sully

43

and Binkley and the fans said, you're my boy. I recommended that the club sign you and bring you right up and I'd do the same thing again. The way it's turned out, though, you may be better off down here. Don't get yourself messed up with any idea you've been abused, kid, you hear!"

"I'm not sore because Mister Sully sent me down here," Stub said. He was thinking of the mediocre exhibition of catching put out last night. "I want to play ball. The quicker I can prove that I'm good enough to play for the Goliaths the better. I figure a fellow can show his stuff in any league—if he gets the chance."

"Right." Selder nodded. A glint of approval was in his eyes as he looked at the youngster. Then he asked a question that caught Stub a little off balance. "Did you bring your catching gear?"

"Why—why, of course! I brought the fielding glove the Goliaths supplied me, too. They owed me that much." Stub eyed Selder curiously. "What's with wanting to know whether I brought my catching gear?"

"Do you still fancy yourself as a catcher?" Selder answered Stub's question with one of his own. Then he added another. "Do you still figure you'd have a better chance to play big-league ball behind the bat?"

"It's for sure I haven't changed my feeling about *that!*"

"Okay, kid. I'll make a deal with you. I'll see to it that you're listed on the club roster as a catcher. I'll promise that you'll get a real chance to work behind the plate. Your end of the deal will be to come out to the ball yard a little early when I say and chase fungoes and honestly try to put into practice tips I give you on playing outfield."

"Man, you've got a deal!" Stub grinned. "Just give me a shot at that catching job! If I don't handle it better than it was taken care of last night, I'll throw away my mitt, shin guards, mask, and chest protector!"

"You'll get a shot at the job. No use stalling around. You'll be behind the dish tonight."

Then Selder frowned a little. "I'm going to level with you," he said. "You take it the right way, now, you hear? The fact is that I have direct orders from the Goliath front office to use you behind the plate. I kind of tricked you into the deal. You can back out of the outfield part, if you want."

"I *don't* want. Look, I haven't forgotten the arguments you gave me on outfielders having a much longer professional-life expectancy than catchers. The constant stooping a catcher does gets his knees and slows him faster. He runs more risk of injury like broken fingers from foul tips or maybe broken bones from crashing runners barging into him trying to score. You're probably right. But after the miserable showing I made trying to play outfield up there —well, you can't blame a fellow for wondering whether he *could* become an outfielder!"

"You can play outfield, kid, make no mistake about that. A man has to have the desire, though, before he can play anything. I played a little outfield in my day and I've been coaching young outfielders five years. I'll stake my reputation that you can play outfield."

Stub shrugged. He did not pursue the topic. Again his blue eyes held curiosity when he asked Selder another question. "Speaking of coaching, how does it happen the Goliaths let you loose? Or if that's none of my business, say so."

"I don't mind your asking, kid. I suppose it seems funny to others, too." Selder was silent a moment. Then he said, "I'll level with you. Sully wanted me fired. He gave the general manager a lot of silly tommyrot that I was after his job, that Milt Binkley and I were in cahoots to get the fans on his neck so bad that the club would have to oust him. He made an issue and, of course, I wouldn't stay with a man as coach who had lost confidence in me.

"I've been wanting a crack at managing. So the front office brought the manager of the Dees up as Goliath third-base coach and gave me the managership down here. It may turn out that I'll be a great big nothing as a manager. I have some ideas I want to try and they may be all wet. Still, if I flop, it won't be because I didn't give the job all I have, you hear!"

Country Selder told the Dees squad much the same at the pre-game meeting. He finished with a promise and a prediction.

"You're all young, mostly in your first year of pro baseball, and you all believed you had the stuff to play baseball for a living or you wouldn't have signed professional contracts. I watched the game last night. Some of you are well along toward developing a losing complex. That stops right now! Some of you just went through the motions. I promise you this: any man who can't get with it and give the club his best efforts will find a blue slip and transportation back home coming his way mighty quick.

"There just isn't any excuse for this ball club to be taking five- and six-run shellackings. We've got some pitchers who throw hard. We have some men who stand up at the plate and take cuts like real hitters. You all get with it and give me the best baseball you own and I predict the Dees will leave the league cellar in a hurry!"

Stub Alison donned his catching mitt for the infield workout. He kept up a running fire of pepper talk. He whipped the ball to bases with plenty of zing behind the pegs. It felt good to be wearing the big mitt again. And it felt good to warm up the starting pitcher while the other team took infield workout.

It felt better to crouch behind the first batter and size him up. Open stance, feet maybe a little too far apart for good balance. Close to the plate edge of the batter's box. Stub signed for a fast ball. He made a target of his mitt which called for the pitch to come high and down the inside lane of the strike zone.

The batter took the pitch. The umpire bellowed, "Strike!"

"The way to throw that seed!" Stub yelled at his pitcher as he threw him the ball. "Nothing to it. Just keep socking away at the old mitt, big fellow!"

The Dees' pitcher was a broad-shouldered, husky right-hander. He had plenty of speed and this night his control was good and his fast ball smoked up there alive. He placed his pitches very near where Stub called. The first batter rolled a weak handle hit to third base and was easily thrown out.

The big pitcher removed the next two men to bat, one on strikes and the other from an easy fly lifted into short center.

At their turn at bat, however, the Dees had to cope with

a fine young left-hander who was in this lowly league only because of wildness. He was very tough to hit when he had control, and he had it tonight. The Dees also went down in order.

The first inning set a pattern for the whole game. A growing murmur rolled through the stands as inning after inning passed with neither team mounting a real scoring threat. It was apparent that the fans liked this tight pitcher's battle after wallowing through so many loosely played, high-scoring games.

Stub Alison was lead-off batter in the bottom of the seventh inning. He had hit the ball both previous times at bat, but neither time really solid. This time he worked the count to three-and-two before getting a pitch he liked. His bat flashed around in a smooth, level swing. He caught the ball a little out in front. It was a white streak past the frantic dive of the first baseman, hit the turf barely inches inside the right foul line, and skipped to the corner. Stub went into second with a stand-up double.

It seemed that Stub's ripping smash upset the southpaw. He lost his control momentarily and walked the Dees' pitcher, attempting to keep the ball high to prevent the big Dees chucker from bunting. Now, Country Selder hung out the sacrifice sign again. The batter laid a twisting bunt that stayed fair along the first-base line. He was thrown out. Stub and the pitcher each moved up a base.

They died on second and third.

The southpaw bore down and forced a batter to go after a hopping fast ball and pop out to short. Then the left-hander blazed a called third strike past the next hitter.

"We'll get to him," Stub said in the dugout as he fastened a shin-guard strap. "All we have to do is keep turning back their hitters."

The big right-hander turned back rival batters in the top of the eighth. Dees hitters rapped the southpaw hard in their half of the inning but the classy left-hander bore down in the clutch and escaped run damage. The Dees right-hander mowed down two batters on strikes in the ninth and the third popped weakly to first base.

"Here's where we win it!" Stub swung two bats in the on-deck circle and yelled at his teammates. "Here's where we take this fork-hander apart!"

They did not exactly take the left-hand star apart, and Stub was not in on the run that finally won the game. The first batter grounded out. Stub drove the right fielder to the wall but the ball was pulled down for just a long out. Country Selder played the percentages and sent a pinch hitter to bat for the pitcher.

The strategy paid off. The pinch hitter drew a base on balls.

A second man refused to fish for pitches barely outside the strike zone and worked the southpaw for free transportation to first. A man was in position to score on a hit now, two out. The left-hander seemed safely out of the inning when he got the next batter to go after an outside pitch.

A little dribbling roller trickled to the first baseman. The pitcher ran over to cover first base, caught the ball tossed to him from the infielder—and missed a stab at the bag with his foot.

With two out, the base runners, of course, were running from the instant bat and ball connected. It may have been Country Selder's little lecture before the game. At any rate, the base runners were really digging. The winning—and only—run was scored from second on the pitcher's error.

"Maybe not the most satisfying way to win a ball game," Selder observed in the dressing room, "but we'll take it! A gift win shows as big in the standings as a game hammered out with big hitting. And we beat the toughest pitcher in the league. This ball club is on the way, you hear, everybody!"

The Dees did not win every game for their new manager. However, they made fans happy by sweeping one series, winning three games of another, and slowing the league leaders by taking three of a five-game set before the club left Dees Field on a road trip.

Stub Alison became a firm fixture behind the plate. He learned more and more about his pitchers and how to handle them, and they learned to depend on his judgment. The stocky rookie studied the hitters of other clubs. They never received a second time the type pitch that they clobbered once. And Stub's bat continued to be a potent factor in his team's attack.

The Dees moved upward in the league standings. When they took three of four of the first road series, they moved quietly into the first division. Stub knew without conceit that he was contributing as much, or more, than anybody to the success of Country Selder's first managing venture.

Since each player expected some day to move up to the

parent Goliaths, all of the Dees followed Goliath games through the sports sheet. Country Selder and Stub Alison read every word pertaining to Mule Sully's club. The Goliaths were not doing so well. And one Saturday, when the Dees played a twi-night double-header, Selder did not give the youngster quite as stiff a workout chasing fungoes in left field. In fact, the manager called a halt a half-hour before other players were due to show up. They sat on the bullpen bench in left field, shaded by the fence.

"Now, kid, you be sure to take this right," Selder said. "This is the last outfield workout, at least for a while. You've improved a hundred per cent. I'd bet that you'd give a good account of yourself if Sully should call you back up. Ninety-nine managers in a hundred would have kept you up there with the hot bat you had, if only for pinch hitting. Sully sure could use your hitting. You're big league, kid, right now. You hear?"

Stub felt warm and good. Country Selder did not hand out praise unless he meant it.

"Yeah, the Goliaths sure could use your bat," Selder drawled. "Looks like they just can't shake out of their latest slump. Sully was as wrong to gamble on that club holding up for one more good season as he was to send you down to spite me. Maybe that isn't right, the ball club is still sound on paper and reputation. They might produce, given the right— Well, let it go. One thing I figure though, kid: the way things are, you're maybe better off down here."

CHAPTER SIX

Up to the Big League Again

The city in which the Dees played the second series of the road trip was many, many miles from the city of the Goliaths. Yet it was a city tourists came to from all over the country. Newspapers from almost every metropolitan area were available on weekends. Stub found a *Gazette* at the newsstand in the lobby of the hotel where the Dees were quartered. Eagerly he turned to the sports section. A mournful headline bannered across the first page.

GOLIATHS LOSE EIGHTH IN ROW! TWELVE OF LAST THIRTEEN!

"Did someone say he thought he saw a 'puddycat' out Goliath Stadium way? Well, he didn't, my friends. The Bears, who opened a series at the stadium yesterday, may be toothless doormats for the rest of the league. Indeed, one might have expected our once-

mighty Goliaths to feast at last on Bear meat. But the harmless 'puddycats' didn't read their script that way.

"*Eight to three was the final score. The Bears scored the eight.*

"*The collection of ballplayers—or should it be put men wearing Goliath uniforms?—no longer than last season battled right down to the wire before losing the pennant to the Savages. Two seasons ago our Goliaths practically made a shambles of the race and emerged world champions after soundly whipping the hated Rebels of the other league. Yesterday this same gang exhibited extreme meekness, not to say apathy, in lying down early and playing dead for the Bears.*

"*Lettering across Goliath shirts should perhaps be changed to P-Y-G-M-I-E-S. There can be no doubt that Sully's Slipping Sluggers have now slipped to such depth that it is well-nigh hopeless to expect other than a dismal finish.*

"*True it is that more than half the season remains to be played. True it is that one may delve into the record book and come up with several clubs that fought up from deep in the standings to win a pennant. The classic example is, of course, the 1914 Boston Braves. George Stallings built a fire under a club that was dead last on the Fourth of July and managed them to a National League pennant and kept going to sweep one of Connie Mack's great Philadelphia Athletics clubs in the World Series.*

"*Alas, this corner holds that Mule Sully can by no*

stretch of imagination resemble a George Stallings. We are beginning to suspect that Sully has mismanaged the club until any manager who succeeds him faces a gigantic job of rebuilding: personnel, morale, fundamental baseball play. The question is:

"WHY DOESN'T GOLIATH BRASS GET HEP THAT MULE SULLY MUST GO?"

Stub stared at the capitalized question. Man, Milt Binkley's piece was really something! The boy picked up the phone and called Country Selder's room. Selder answered almost immediately.

"Stub Alison here," the rookie said. "I bought a *Gazette* awhile ago. My gosh, you ought to see the stuff in the sports section about the Goliaths and Mister Sully!"

"I've seen it, kid. I was just about to phone you. There are some things I'd like to mull over and I mull things over better when I have someone to talk aloud to. Can you meet me in the lobby and go along and be a kind of talking horse?"

"I'll be right there."

Country Selder came from the elevator shortly after Stub occupied a lobby chair. The manager looked casually around, then motioned the stocky youngster. Outside, Selder said, "Didn't see any of the boys and I suppose it doesn't really matter, but this thing has me tied up so I'd just as soon none of the other boys would—would—well, I'd just as soon they didn't know that I know any more than is in the *Gazette*."

Stub glanced curiously at the older man but made no

comment. This was probably what Selder meant by saying that he mulled things over better talking them out. Okay, let him go on mulling. As of that moment, Stub had no idea at all what he was talking about.

"The business up there has been snowballing since you and I left the Goliaths," Selder went on. "Not that our leaving had anything special to do with it. My wife sends me the *Gazette* sports sheet every day by air mail. Binkley has been sniping at Sully and printing cracks that Sully makes about him and the *Gazette*—ones that Bink hears about, that is. Bink's stuff that Mrs. Selder sends is a day late but he phoned me last night and I bought a *Gazette* first thing this morning."

Stub looked quickly at Selder as the older man momentarily stopped speaking. He did not ask any questions. It wasn't long before Selder continued. A frown wrinkled Selder's rugged features and he seemed to be talking more to himself than to Stub.

"I don't think Bink has ever been so stirred up. And according to him, the publisher of the *Gazette* is just as mad. He owns a sizable block of stock in the Goliath Baseball Company and swings a lot of influence. Yet I wonder if Bink isn't a little overboard in asking if I'd take the job managing the Goliaths when they fire Sully sometime in the next ten days!"

Country Selder walked a half-dozen strides, seemingly lost in thought. He let out a breath.

"What a foolish question! Bink ought to know it's been my ambition ever since I began to slow up as a player to manage some day the only club I ever signed a major-league contract with! But all the same, even if Bink has inside dope and knows for sure that Sully is on the way out, any offer for me to go back up there and manage the ball club has to come from the general manager.

"I don't know why I stalled and didn't tell Bink that. I'm going back to the hotel and put in a long-distance call and tell him now. All this is strictly between you and me, kid, you hear?"

Stub nodded. His own pulse had quickened and for an instant he wondered why he should become excited over what happened to Mule Sully, or Country Selder. Then, abruptly, he knew that it was not the imminent return of Selder to the beleaguered Goliaths that had caused his pulse to quicken.

It was Country Selder who had persuaded the Goliaths to sign a fellow named Alison. This fellow was Selder's boy, and hadn't Selder told him only yesterday that he was big league right now? It was only reasonable to presume that if and when Selder moved into the managership of the Goliaths, Stub Alison would go along back to the big league.

The situation between Sully and the Goliath front-office bosses and Milt Binkley and the *Gazette* came to a sudden and dramatic head well within the ten days Binkley had mentioned to Selder. The news came over all wire services Tuesday night. It was carried in more or less detail by every paper subscribing to any news service. Stub read the heading in the morning paper—

GOLIATH MANAGER RESIGNS UNDER FIRE.

In the body of the newspaper piece were two statements that tended to show the writer of the headline was unfair, at least on the surface. One statement was from Sully's personal physician. The other was from the Goliath club physician. Both stated that extensive examination, X rays, and laboratory tests gave conclusive evidence that to continue under the tension of managing a big-league ball club might seriously damage Sully's health. Neither doctor would make further diagnosis, but both agreed that Sully suffered from an extremely serious ailment.

The news-service wires also carried a companion piece to the resignation of Sully. It appeared in the same column of the paper Stub read.

DEES TO LOSE MANAGER?

"Nothing definite could be obtained by questioning Goliath officials and Country Selder refused any statement other than no comment. The hot rumor in baseball circles, however, is that Country Selder will return to take over as Goliath field boss."

Country Selder phoned Stub in midmorning.

"I've just talked with the general manager by phone," Selder said. "I'm it. I'm catching a noon flight and taking Pat Monahan with me to be third-base coach. The farm director is shuffling managers so there will be a man to handle the Dees tonight but their former manager will be with some other club. He didn't want to stay on as coach under me.

"There isn't much doubt that Mule Sully is suffering from a brain tumor although the fact hasn't been officially given out. I feel a little like a heel for holding some of the feeling that I've held toward Mule. He hasn't been a well man for a long time, it seems."

There was a short silence. Then Selder went on.

"The reason I'm phoning you is this: as soon as I can arrange for the Dees to get a catcher to replace you, we'll bring you up to the Goliaths! Take care of yourself, kid, and don't get hurt, you hear me!"

"I hear you!" Stub all but yelled into the phone. "Zowie!"

He almost asked if he would be brought up as a catcher. Of course, he would. He'd proved to Selder that he *was* a catcher. The main thing was that Stub Alison was going up to the big league again!

CHAPTER SEVEN

Rookies Don't Always Star

Country Selder was a busy man. He took charge of the Goliaths the day before the annual All-Star game break in the schedule. The one game that he watched his charges lose convinced Selder that things had deteriorated even more than Milt Binkley had said.

"We're hurting in several spots," Selder told the general manager. "Banyan and Fox either have slowed tremendously or they aren't putting out up to par. They just are not making the double play like a keystone combination has to for a winning club.

"Our pitching is sour. Molton seems way past his peak and Mike Clancy isn't hitting the size of his hat. Clancy never was exactly a bulwark of defense out there in the field and without his hitting he is more of a liability than an asset."

"You lay things on the line." The general manager

shrugged. "Not that we haven't been aware of some of our shortcomings. We're ready and anxious to strengthen the club. There is money available to purchase talent. We're open for trades. But—"

The general manager spread his hands.

"The 'but' is the trouble," he said. "Talk trade with other clubs and they only want to talk about Samron or Kendrick or Ryder or some of our top prospects on farm teams. There just simply is not the kind of talent we need available for purchase, no matter how large your bankroll is. Have you talked with the director of Farm Clubs?"

Selder nodded. "We have some fine young players coming up through the farm system," he said. "The majority, though, are from a year to three years away from being ready for the top. Also, there is the matter of alienating fans in the farm-club cities. They would be bitter if we grabbed their best men when some of them are in the midst of hot pennant fights. Besides all that, it is always a gamble to put too much of a burden on rookies."

The general manager said, "Officials of practically every major-league club will be at the All-Star game. We'll make all the contacts we can. We may be able to come up with some help. I tell you frankly, though, Selder, the chances are slim. It's increasingly true as competition for talent grows keener: a club just about has to depend on developing its own talent. I'd say that you're apt to have to make do with the personnel we have."

Stub Alison expected a telephone call or wire every day. None came. The All-Star break passed. The new Dees manager was not a Country Selder but he was a competent baseball man and the momentum the young club had engendered under Selder kept them rolling.

Doggone it, Stub thought after a week had passed since Selder departed. What's holding up production? This club is on the beam. Pitchers have learned pretty much what to pitch to the tough hitters to get them out most often. Anybody who can stand back there and hold up the pitches can catch. Why doesn't Selder send somebody down here?

It was four days later that the wire came. A catcher would report to the Dees in time for the game that night. Stub Alison would find a seat reserved for him on the first flight for the city in which the Goliaths were playing.

Selder's club was not playing at a pennant-winning pace, but they were showing some improvement. They had won five and lost seven of the dozen games played under Selder. One new player had been secured on waivers from the Rebels in the other league. His name was Layne. He was not young as ballplayers go but neither was he as ancient as some of the Goliath veterans.

"I figure I've got anyway two years more of big-league ball in my system," he told Country Selder. "Maybe more, if I get a chance to play regularly. Sitting on the bench is what's killed me."

Selder put the new man in right field. The manager pulled no punches with Mike Clancy. "You've slowed to a walk out there," he said. "Balls hit to right that should be putouts drop too often for hits, and drives that good fielding would hold to singles are going for extra bases."

"Blast it, Country, you can't do this to me! We played together! You know I can sock that ball. You need my power!"

"You're hitting .240, Clancy. Granted that every once in a blue moon you get hold of one and ride it out of the park. It isn't done often enough to warrant keeping a .240 hitter who doesn't get off the nickel in the field in the lineup!"

"I'm not washed up, Selder! You can't say I'm all done. I'll make you eat your words!"

"You're out of the lineup for now," Selder said firmly. "A rest may do you good. You'll have chances to pinch hit. Whenever you show me you can help the club more in the lineup than out, you'll be back in!"

Stub Alison reported to the Goliaths the day Clancy was benched. Country Selder greeted him, told the youngster to grab his fielder's glove, and work out in left.

"Left field!" Stub looked incredulous. "Not that again! My gosh, are you going to give me the same run-around that Mister Sully gave me? Haven't I proved that I'm a catcher?"

"You can catch, kid. I never said you couldn't. I've got DeMino and Dahl and they can catch, too. Unless you want to be bullpen catcher—and I don't know what we'd do with Pete then—you'd better make up your mind to like playing outfield!"

The youngster found that it was different in left field than it had been before. Somehow he had an easy confidence. This ball park was not like Goliath Stadium. Stands completely surrounded the playing field. The roof line was level except for the narrow bleacher section in deep center field. But the rookie did not think he would have much trouble in any outfield after the hours he had spent with Country Selder.

He caught three routine drives that game and snagged one, after a long run, that had been labeled extra bases. The catch cut off two enemy runs. At the end of the game it was not his fielding that bothered Stub Alison.

He had gone to the plate four times. Not once did he come close to getting a hit. He had the four-for-oh day. And it was a pitcher whose stuff he had clobbered earlier in the season that hung the horse collar on him.

The Goliaths won the game when Ark Molton homered in the ninth after Schmidt worked the pitcher for a walk and Layne, the newcomer from the Rebels, singled Schmidt to third. The 6 to 5 win had been well earned and the Goliath dressing room was filled with boisterous chatter. Ark Molton naturally felt especially good. Maybe it was because the big first baseman figured that Alison was responsible for Clancy riding the bench that Molton jabbed the needle.

"You go four-for-four today?" Ark asked the rookie.

Stub did not look up. He knew that Molton was well aware that he had been shut out of the hit column. He felt low enough. And he had vowed that he wasn't going to get into another hassle with the veterans. He just shook his head.

"Why, they must have robbed you!" Molton pretended surprise. "We worn-out has-beens have been looking forward to your bat showing us the way!"

Stub flushed. A biting retort came to him. He shut his lips tight.

The Goliath rookie left fielder failed to get a hit the next day.

In the series finale, Alison made it thirteen official at bats without a base hit. He managed only a base on balls in five trips to the plate.

He was not surprised when Country Selder told him before the opening game in the Redbirds park that Layne would move to left and Mike Clancy would be in right field.

"Big Mike came through twice pinch hitting," Selder said. "I promised he'd have another chance if he could produce. Maybe he's mad enough at me to keep going. Anyway, you're way off, kid. There's nothing wrong with you up at the plate that I can spot. As usual, when a man falls into a hitting slump, everything that you really hit square goes straight at a fielder. I think maybe you're trying too hard. Relax and take it easy on the bench for a couple of days."

The "couple of days" stretched on and on. Layne seemed to have taken a new lease on life with the change of leagues. Big Mike Clancy still allowed balls to fall safely in right field and he did not bat a thousand. But he did resemble the Clancy of a year or two ago, the dangerous power hitter who carried the potential to break up a ball game any time he was at bat.

Nobody doubted that the Goliaths were a better club than they had been under Mule Sully. They were playing much better ball. Still, as July ended and the hot summer days began to take the usual toll, the Goliaths were barely at .500 in the standings. They shuttled in and out of the first division every few days. Selder sent Alison up as a pinch hitter on several occasions that called for left-hand batting.

The rookie did not start any fires with his bat. It was once when he flied out to leave two mates on base that the youngster all but forgot his vow to stay out of rhubarbs with the veterans. Ark Molton sounded off when Stub returned to the dugout.

"You'd think," Ark sneered, "that a guy who shot off his bazoo the way a certain party did and then fumbles a second chance to deliver when it's handed to him, ought to tumble that he's just not big league!"

"Yeah." Mike Clancy grunted agreement. "Even a fresh kid that's so free with comments about his betters ought to see the writing on the wall when it's ten feet tall!"

"There are some alleged ballplayers cut from bush-league cloth and that's all," Banyan said. "Could we have a case in point with us?"

Stub managed to keep his mouth shut. Truthfully, he was so low in spirit that he wondered if maybe Banyan's remark might be true. I wish they would send me back to the Dees, he thought. I wish—oh, knock it off! Who are you trying to kid? You know doggone well you'd give anything to shake out of the dumps and help Selder make a showing with this club.

The rookie did not know that he was one of the main topics in an interview that Selder gave Milt Binkley after that game. The sports writer asked for frank stuff, promised that he would print nothing that Selder marked confidential.

"We helped ourselves in acquiring Layne," the manager said. "I'd have to reserve judgment whether he can maintain the pace he's set for us so far. I hope he can. But some of it may be due to the fact that it's our league's pitcher's first time around the track with him. They could cool him off later.

"Benching Clancy helped him. I didn't believe when I benched him that Mike was completely through. Definitely he is on the downhill side of his career, but Big Mike can still win a ball game for you. Molton has improved. The defense around second base is better since I gave Banyan and Fox the word. I warned them that I'd bring up a second-base combination we have on a farm club if they didn't shake out of it. If we're going to lose ball games because of lousy second-base play, we might as well be giving some untried kids the experience. With all this, the fact remains that the club is not playing pennant-winning ball."

Binkley shot a quick look at the manager. The sports writer said, "Do you honestly feel that the Goliaths have potential to win the pennant, Country?"

Country Selder hesitated. When he spoke it was in a slow drawl. "Let's put it this way: any major-league ball club has the potential to put together winning streaks if everything clicks. Let a ball club get going on a winning streak and they can catch fire. Give the Goliath personnel something—and I wish I knew what to give them—to bring out their top play and—well, I can say honestly that with the proper spark provided, we could catch fire and take it all!"

"How about Stub Alison, Country? He fired the team before Sully sent him down. Could the rookie provide the spark again?"

"Anybody or anything could provide the spark." Selder evaded a direct answer. "I haven't given up on Alison. I still believe he's a solid prospect to develop into a dependable big-league ballplayer, and like I said before, maybe a great one. Right now he's in a bad slump and hasn't been able to shake it. Give him two or three base hits and he could snap out of the slump and go on a batting streak."

Selder stopped speaking a moment and frowned. He eyed the sports writer. He said, "This is strictly off the record, Bink. Other managers in the league share my convictions on the kid. Our front office has overtures for trades involving Alison and I'm having a little trouble fighting them off, the way he's been going.

"The Hoppers offer a couple of players that we could use right now, probably better than Alison. They just won't listen to any deal that doesn't include the kid. But I have a strong feeling that trading Alison off would murder me sooner or later."

Selder drew in a breath, frowned momentarily, then let it out. "I'm keeping the kid for now, anyway," he said. "Maybe his bat will come alive again and he'll spark the club. Right now the biggest thing Alison has to realize is that rookies don't always star. Then it's up to him to take it from there."

CHAPTER EIGHT

Almost Traded

The Goliaths continued to play in-and-out ball through early August. Country Selder did everything he could think of to goad the club into a sustained winning streak. He got on Ark Molton about being overweight. He needled Fox and Banyan by getting Binkley to run a rumor in his column that the Goliaths were waiting anxiously until the season closed Labor Day for the farm club that the promising shortstop-second baseman duo played on. The inference was clear that the youngsters would replace Fox and Banyan.

Selder praised pitchers when he figured they responded to praise. He talked bluntly and sharply to any pitcher who turned in a lazy or lackadaisical exhibition. The Goliaths were in fifth place at the start of the final week in August. But they were only a half game behind the Bucks in fourth place and a game and a half back of the Redbirds in third spot. They were nine full games behind the Hoppers and Savages, tied for the league lead.

"There is just something lacking," Selder said to Binkley in an interview before the Bears opened a Goliath home stand. "Blame it, Bink, I'm not getting all I should out of this ball club!"

"That's your opinion." Binkley shook his head. "Personally, I think you're getting more out of the club than there is there, which may sound screwy. What I mean is that they're playing over their heads right now."

"You're wrong, Bink. There is plenty of baseball left in these guys."

"Why don't you get a real bat and beat yourself over the head instead of a word-stuffed one?" Binkley again shook his head. "You know as well as I do that Sully was blinded to the fact that a once-powerful baseball machine needed some replacement parts. You finish in the first division this year, get yourself some replacements for two-three spots, and you'll be in the pennant fight from the getaway next season."

"This isn't next season, and I can't go along with you that we're realizing our potential."

Binkley shoved a thumb against his hatbrim. "I keep coming back to the Alison youngster," he said. "Layne hasn't fallen clear out of the batting-average column, but you sure had it doped that pitchers might cool him off. Aren't you about ready to give Alison another shot? Maybe a rest would help Layne."

"Maybe," Selder said. "I've been watching the kid closely. Some days he looks sharp up there at the plate in batting practice. Then when I send him in to pinch hit, he tightens and falls flat on his kisser."

Milt Binkley drummed his fingers on the battered desk top. He looked up at Country Selder and a half-grin pulled a corner of his mouth higher.

"There's been a bee buzzing around in my alleged brain for quite a while," Binkley said. "You'll probably give me the big laugh. But—well, here it is: stick the rookie in the lineup and tell him beforehand that you want him to stop taking guff from Molton, Clancy, and the rest. Tell him to jab the needle right back like he did before!"

Country Selder stared at the sports writer. The manager's rugged features wrinkled in a scowl.

"Knock it off, Bink," he said. "Are you setting out to give Kendrick a run for his joker title? Kendrick pulled that gag on the kid the first day he wore a Goliath uniform.

"It happens that I'm playing the kid in left tomorrow. The Hoppers want him badly enough that they've increased their offer by another player and they'll throw in a top farm-club player. The front office is pushing me for a decision. I want a good look at the kid in several games before I give it. If you're serious about that needling thing, you're crazy!"

"It's an occupational hazard of sports writing." Binkley nodded. "Do you have any objections if I talk to Alison?"

"I most certainly do!" Country Selder left no doubt of his feeling. He eyed Binkley levelly. "I'm not fooling, Bink. I run my ball club. You say as much as one word to the kid along that line and I'll have your hide! You hear?"

Stub Alison took his cuts at the plate in batting practice next day. He always had his swings at the plate. He also worked out catching fungo flies in left field. That was nothing out of the ordinary, either. He'd done it every day since coming back to the club.

At first he had looked every day at the batting order Selder always taped to the end of the dugout, hoping against hope that he would find his name, that Selder had just forgotten to tell him he was playing. He hadn't done that for quite a while. Today he took his usual seat at the far end of the dugout.

"There sure is one spot on this bench that's well polished," Ark Molton said. He flicked a sidewise glance at the rookie. "My, my, who would ever have thought it!"

Stub flushed. He'd had enough. He was just about to let loose on the big first baseman when Country Selder barked from outside the dugout. "Alison! You're in left today!"

Stub jerked a quick gaze to the manager.

Selder said, "Get with it, kid!"

Molton's barb was forgotten. Stub raced from the dugout leading the Goliaths when the umpire called, "Play!"

He did not have a fielding chance that inning. He consulted the batting order when he came in. Layne had been hitting in the sixth spot behind Molton. Selder had not changed the order.

"Well, there'll be nothing to it now." Mike Clancy stood looking at the batting order after Stub turned away. "With the big-stuff rook hitting in the middle of the order, all us old gaffers need to do is to get on base!"

In all probability the needling would have stopped right there if Country Selder had been in the dugout, but one week of bench managing had proved all Selder could take. He sent Pat Monahan to coach first base, relieved Pete Hagan of the coaching job, and told Peter he could devote full time to being bullpen catcher. Country Selder was back coaching third base so he did not hear Clancy.

Stub stared silently at the burly slugger for a moment. Then the rookie sucked in a deep breath and turned quickly away. He knew that he had reached the limit of taking barbs without handing them back.

The Goliaths mounted a scoring threat in their half of the inning. Fox crowded the plate, worked the count to three-and-two then fouled off four pitches too close to the strike zone to take. He finally earned a base on balls. Rog Samron promptly sent Fox to third by singling sharply to right. Schmidt, Clancy, Molton—the long ball power of the batting order—were the next three hitters. Country Selder went for the big inning. He passed Schmidt the hit-away sign instead of signaling a sacrifice bunt.

Schmidt topped a sinker. The ball hopped down the first-base line. It was not sharply hit. The first baseman dashed in and fielded the roller, took one look to see that Country Selder held Fox at third. There was no chance to get the fleet Samron at second but a snap throw to the pitcher, covering the first-base sack, nipped Schmidt.

Mike Clancy had three lusty cuts. He drove a ball into the twenty-second row in the left-field stands—foul by eight feet. Then he missed a high, hard one for the third strike.

Two out. Ark Molton strode menacingly to the plate. Selder yelled from the coaching box, "Only two out, Ark, bust one!"

Ark Molton thought he had a curve gauged just right to "bust one." His bat lashed around, but the pitcher had a little more stuff on the bender than Ark figured. The ball sliced off the bat. It looked like a safe hit just out of reach between first and second.

The second baseman never gave up on the ball. He dived the final six feet, speared the ball in the webbing of his glove, tumbled completely head over heels, and came up in position to throw. He put all he had behind the throw. It seemed that ball and Molton arrived at the same time. The umpire called Molton out.

It was a very close play and Molton made token protest. He did not press it, though, because he knew that he had been thrown out by an eyelash. Pat Monahan, first-base coach, simply turned and walked to the dugout.

Man, that Molton is slowest of the slow, Stub thought. He runs forever in one place! The rookie said nothing aloud. Ark Molton did not return the favor.

Alison was leadoff batter in the bottom of the second inning. He swung a couple of bats in front of the dugout to loosen his shoulder muscles while the Bear pitcher threw warmup tosses. Ark Molton looked toward the end of the dugout where the rookie had been sitting so many days.

"What, nobody keeping the polished spot shiny today!"

Molton looked around. Then he pretended that he had forgotten Stub was in the lineup when he saw the youngster swinging bats. "Oh, sure," Molton said. "I forgot our best bench polisher took a day off to pull the splinters out of his pants!"

Stub eyed the first baseman. The rookie's tone was a soft drawl when he spoke.

"You're straining pretty hard to be pretty unfunny, I'd say. It might be better to let things lay, Molton!"

"Let what lay, Rook? Can't a man make a simple observation without you lipping off?"

Stub Alison went to bat thinking more about Molton's silly needling than about trying to get out of his batting slump. There could have been nothing wrong with his reflexes. He stepped into the first pitch. His bat lashed around in a smooth, level swing and he met the ball solidly on the good wood. A drive sizzled between first and second never over six feet off the ground. A "clothesline" hit, a "frozen rope" in player parlance.

Stub was forced out by Banyan. DeMino flied out. Kendrick fanned. But the stocky youngster felt good when he took his place in left field. He still felt good when he came in. He had judged a line drive down the foul line perfectly and raced over to make a putout of a ball that could easily have gone for a triple.

Stub still felt good when he came into the dugout. It was not in his mind to rekindle the word warfare. It was Mike Clancy who started the rhubarb.

"This'll be the inning," Clancy said. "Three men get on; Clancy and Molton, worn-out gaffers that they are, leave the bags crowded for Big Stuff. Accidents do happen twice in a row and the mouthy rookie will really belt one. Four markers for our side!"

"Sure," Ark Molton agreed. "Country's just been keeping him bench-polishing to fool the other clubs! He's really Selder's secret weapon!"

The Bear pitcher had been having control trouble. He did not get it straightened out. He issued bases on balls to Fox, Samron, and Schmidt. Mike Clancy walloped an almost-grand slam homer—but the ball was caught just before it would have cleared the barrier in left. Fox scored after the catch.

Ark Molton started for the plate. Stub Alison moved into the on-deck circle. The rookie cupped his hands and gave Molton a bit of unasked-for advice.

"If you hit it, try running it out this time. Man, if you're getting too old to drag that fat carcass around fast enough to keep warm, you ought to apply for Social Security and call it a day!"

Molton glared. His lips moved and Stub knew that whatever the slugger was saying was not complimentary. The youngster grinned. Maybe that would shut off the needling.

Ark Molton tied into the second pitch. It was a home run from the instant bat met speeding baseball. Molton followed Samron and Schmidt around the bases. They waited across the plate and gave Molton the traditional handshake. Stub Alison also stuck out his hand. Molton jerked downward and snarled.

"Try that for size, Rook! You ever get so you can blow

one out of the park like that, you'll have a right to lip off!"

Stub grinned. He had no idea of making a prophecy. He said carelessly, "You set a good pattern, all right. It seems as though a fellow ought to be able to follow a pattern."

A relief pitcher came in for the Bears. A leftie, since Alison and Banyan, the next two batters, hit from the first-base side of the plate. Left-handers had never given Stub any particular trouble. He stood outside the batter's box, watching the warmup pitches, timing them. The ball looked as big as a basketball.

Stub had the hit sign from Selder. He was ready and the first pitch was right in his groove. He made a much faster one out of a fast ball. The drive was not a towering hit as Molton's had been, but it was perfectly timed and carried every ounce of the youngster's stocky bulk behind it. A fan in the right-center field bleachers reached up and grabbed himself a souvenir. Stub trotted around the bases.

It was his first major-league home run. It was good. The slap on the seat of the britches that Selder gave him passing third was good. Everything was good.

"It was a nice pattern," Stub said in the dugout. He eyed Molton. "We must try it again sometime, huh?"

Molton mumbled beneath his breath, and the needling between Stub and the veterans was off and running again. So was the hitting by Goliath batters. The final score was an easy 12 to 3 win for Duke Kendrick. The dark left-hander made a point of waiting for Stub after the game.

"For a long time," Kendrick said, "I've felt a little on the queasy side about you. Maybe Sully wouldn't have sent you down if I'd never have filled you full of baloney that first day. Maybe you wouldn't have gone into that horrible slump if it—"

"Forget anything like that," Stub interrupted. "Looks as though I've shaken the slump. Four for five today. A fellow couldn't bear any grudge when he had a day like that—and I never blamed you anyway."

That game touched off the longest winning streak the Goliaths had enjoyed in two seasons. They took two more to sweep the Bears. The Hillies came to Goliath Stadium and left two days later, a pair of games worse off in the lost column. Stub Alison fielded his position flawlessly and pounded the ball at the plate. He notched seven base hits and drove in five runs in the four games.

"What's with Alison and the projected trade?" Binkley asked Country Selder. "You said the Hoppers weren't interested unless they could get the youngster in time to be eligible for the World Series. They'd have to have him before September first and this is the last day of August."

"Also it's the last time I'll consider trading the kid— ever." Selder grinned. "The general manager just nixed a deal the Hoppers offered by phone. They added a pretty good pitching prospect to the players they offered before. But wouldn't I be a sucker to trade off Alison? The way the kid is going, he *could* spark us into joining the Hoppers and Savages and Redbirds in the stretch drive for that flag. You hear!"

"Or something!" Binkley seemed amused. "In any case, I presume it's safe to run a line in the column that Alison was just *almost* traded!"

CHAPTER NINE

Bad Breaks in the Stretch Drive

The word war between Stub Alison and the veterans waxed heavier than before. Country Selder would have had to be deaf, blind, and stupid not to have been aware of the continuing rhubarb. Finally he considered taking some action—maybe hand a stiff chewing out to the kid. The trouble was Molton, Clancy, Fox, and Banyan were as bad as the rookie.

The Goliath manager mulled the situation over aloud to Milt Binkley. They were in the privacy of Selder's club-house office. The team had just concluded the home stand. Trunks of equipment were being packed for the final long road trip of the season.

"We'll visit every ball park in the league and wind up against the Hoppers. And here I am starting what could be a vital trip with the kid and half the rest of my team at each other all the time." Selder scowled, then went on. "I'd take the whole bunch over the jumps except for a thing that sticks out with me like a pitcher taking the mound in a catcher's outfit would."

Milt Binkley chuckled. There was a fondness in his eyes as the sports writer looked at Selder.

"Don't tell me," Binkley said. "Let me show off my well-known understanding of the species ballplayer. It's just not in your book to change one teeny thing that might upset the rhythm of winning. Right?"

"I'm an old-timer." Country Selder nodded. "I guess baseball old-timers are alike. A man picks up superstitions along the way. You tell yourself they don't mean a thing but you live with them all the same."

The sports writer chuckled again. He eyed Selder.

"There's something I've been wondering about quite awhile now," Binkley said. "Have you stopped to consider just when your ball club began to really come alive?"

"Of course!" The Goliath manager looked surprised. "We started winning consistently the day the Bears came to the stadium; the day I put Stub Alison back in the lineup."

"And?"

"What do you mean, and?"

"Is that all you noticed?"

"What else was there to notice? What's eating you, Bink?"

"Well, you settled the question I had in mind." Binkley shrugged. "But if you asked my advice—which same I now offer gratis, in case you shouldn't ask—don't chew out Alison for handing Molton and his buddies as good as they jab at him."

The Goliaths held firm grip on third place in the standings as they opened the road trip at the park of the Hillies. Third place was fine. What really steamed up Goliath fans, though, and engendered signs of pennant fever in some of the players, was the fact that the club trailed the second-place Savages only two and a half games. The Savages were a scant half game behind the league-leading Hoppers.

"The schedule favors the Savages and Hoppers in that they finish at home." Selder said in an interview with a sports writer in the city of the Hillies. "We finish on the road. But the Savages and Hoppers don't have this stretch battle for the flag sewed up between them. We're going to be in there right down to the wire. You can quote me on that!"

A sweep of the three games in the Hillies park got the road trip off to a flying start. The previous swing around the league made by the Goliaths had left several games postponed due to rain. One was with the Bears. It had been rescheduled as part of a Saturday double-header.

The Bears beat Duke Hendricks in the first game. The handsome left-hander pitched a four-hitter, but one of the four happened to be a homer with a man on base. The Bear pitcher throttled the hot Goliath bats when hits meant runs except one time. Stub Alison belted his second big-league home run. The rest of the batting order racked up ten solid hits but they could not produce safeties when they were most needed. Outhit twelve to four, the Bears still won the opener 2 to 1 because the payoff comes on runs. Twelve Goliaths left stranded on the bases counted for nothing.

That was the only game of the four that the Bears won. The Goliaths left town in a virtual tie with the Savages, and both clubs had gained a half game on the Hoppers.

The Goliaths moved to Blue Sox Park. They left three days later with an even split in four games. They took two of three from the Bucks. Then they killed what faint hope the Redbirds entertained by sweeping four games played in Bird Field. The club swaggered into the city of the Savages a half game ahead of the local club in the all-important lost column although the Savages had won a game more and clung to second place by a slim seven-percentage points.

All during the road trip Alison and the veterans jabbed the needle.

"Come on, Father Time," Stub yelled at Ark Molton when the first baseman went to bat in the eighth inning of a Bear game. Molton had been handcuffed in three previous trips. "Quit flailing that bat around as though you were swatting flies, and crack one!"

Ark Molton cracked one over the left-field wall. Fox and Schmidt scored ahead of him.

In the final of the Bucks series, the kid needled Mike Clancy about creaky old joints. His next time at bat Clancy slammed a towering drive high into the bleachers in deep center field. Molton attempted to wither the rookie when Clancy smashed the prodigious homer.

"If you ever get so you can bust one like that, you can be satisfied to have creaky old joints!"

"That's about the only way you refugees from Social Security can be sure you won't be thrown out," Stub replied. He grinned. "Maybe you need a dose of the same needle, Grandpa. You're not so spry these days!"

The needling went on every day. The Goliath stretch drive went along with it. The club came into the Tepee—the stadium of the Savages—a different ball club than they had been on previous trips. They were playing hard, aggressive, tough ball. They were playing as though they were hungry to regain prestige lost in losing the pennant last year.

Every sports writer, every radio commentator, all local television stations labeled the four-game Savages-Goliaths series crucial. Crucial may be a much overworked word but there could be no doubt that it was apropos in this instance.

"A split will do us a lot of no good," Binkley said in the press box before the opening game. "We have to take three out of four. We can really kill the Savages by sweeping four. I think we'll do just that!"

"Who-o-o-e-e-e! Listen to the man talk!" A sports writer for a local paper gave Binkley a curious look. "How high can you get on a ball club? Last time you were in town you were down, down, down on your outfit!"

"There've been some changes made." Binkley nodded. For an instant an amused flicker crossed his eyes as though he owned a secret. "Yep, there have been some changes made," he repeated. "Starting with young Alison going out there and showing he can play outfield!"

"He hasn't done so bad with that long war club he swings, either, but the Savages are a good, solid ball club. I can't see your gang sweeping them. Actually, the Goliaths would need more than their share of luck to take three games, I believe."

After the final out was made in the fourth game, Milt Binkley rubbed it into his fellow sports writer.

"Let's see, you claimed we'd need more than our share of luck to take three. Well, maybe the two-hit shutout that Duke Kendrick tossed at you in the opener was luck. I don't know about the even dozen base knocks good for eighteen bases and eight runs that we got. Would that be luck or an explosive ball club producing? Eight to nothing, 7 to 4, 6 to 2, 5 to 1. Never less than a three-run bulge. Maybe we were lucky. One thing is for sure—the Savages are dead!"

"Okay, okay, so you called the shot." The other sports writer grinned. "The Goliaths are the hottest outfit to hit the Tepee this season. I hope they go on and take the flag. I still say that it's good luck when a club avoids slumps or injuries to key men in a race as close as this one. Who-o-o-e-e-e! Hollywood couldn't have come up with a better ending than this pennant race!"

"It would never be believed as fiction," Binkley agreed. "Goliaths and Hoppers tied with eighty-nine wins and sixty-two losses and meeting in the final three games of the schedule. The chips are down for sure!"

It seemed that the good fortune the Goliaths had enjoyed would go on as they scored an unearned run in the top of the ninth in the first game. The run broke a 2 to 2 deadlock that had held for seven innings. Goliath luck continued into the bottom of the ninth.

Rog Samron ran back to the wall and flung his body,

glove high as he could stretch, in a desperate leap. The ball snagged in the webbing of his glove and he held it although he crashed against the barrier. The drive would have been a home run.

The leading hitter of the Savages came to the plate. He ducked back from a high, fast one—and the ball hit his bat. A looping little fly drifted out toward first base. Ark Molton had only to take three steps to catch it. The next hitter undercut the first pitch to him.

Tony DeMino dashed back under the pop foul. It was not too high. DeMino went all out. The ball snuggled in his big mitt just as the veteran catcher's shoulder crashed hard against the concrete facing of the stands. He held the ball.

Doc, Goliath trainer, ran from the dugout. DeMino was grimacing from pain.

"I've done something to my shoulder," the catcher gritted. "Take it easy, Doc!"

DeMino was rushed to the hospital. X rays showed no fracture, but he had a bad shoulder separation. He would not be able to lift his arm, let alone throw a baseball. DeMino would definitely not play again this season.

The Hoppers climbed on Big Pete Ryder early in the second game. Before Selder could get a relief pitcher heated up and in from the bullpen, three Hopper runs were in and the bases loaded. Two of those base runners scored while the relief pitcher worked out of the bad spot. The five runs held up despite a Goliath rally in the eighth inning. Hoppers, 5; Goliaths, 4, were the figures on the scoreboard at the finish.

The clubs were deadlocked for the league lead with one game left to play.

"A schedule from mid-April to September," Milt Binkley held forth in the press box. "One hundred and fifty-three games played. Now it comes down to the whole ball of wax going to the team winning this one game! Our luck had better hold up now!"

A long debate could have been held whether the Goliath luck held out.

True it was that in the final game Lefty Byrnes was lucky to survive wildness that plagued him the first three innings and escape with only one Hopper run scored. It could be set down that the two-base smash off Stub Alison's bat in the Goliath second had an element of luck in that the ball took a bad hop after striking the turf near the foul line in right, and two runs scored when one was the legitimate expectation. It may have been partly luck that enabled the rookie to snatch a high foul right out of the hands of a fan in a field box and squelch a Hopper threat.

There could be no argument that the foul tip that caught Jake Dahl's meat hand in the bottom of the eighth was bad luck.

Dahl said no word, shook it off, waved Doc back to the dugout when the trainer started toward him. Dahl gave no evidence that he had a broken finger on his throwing hand while he caught for the last two batters.

The finger was badly swollen and beginning to blacken when Doc probed gently in the dressing room.

"It's busted, there's no doubt," Doc said. "We win the

ball game and the pennant—but we lose the services of Jake!"

Country Selder gave out a statement to the sports writers an hour after the game.

> *"We make no attempt to minimize the importance of losing DeMino and Dahl. But the Goliaths will show up in Rebel Stadium next Tuesday to open the World Series. We are not automatically presenting the Rebels the world championship. We concede them nothing.*
>
> *"Alison will be behind the plate for us. Alison caught for me in a minor league. Alison will do the job.*
>
> *"Don't put this down as mere whistling to keep up our courage. Actually, if our catching staff had to be cut down, it is better for a new catcher to take over now than in the regular schedule. Scouting reports on Rebel hitters have been compiled. Alison will learn as much about the other league hitters from the reports as Dahl or DeMino could have learned.*
>
> *"I am confident that Goliath catching will be adequate for World Series play."*

Milt Binkley read the copy of Selder's statement that was given to him. The sports writer shoved his hat higher on his head.

"I hope you're right, Country," he said. "I'm for the rookie one hundred per cent and all the way. But it sure is tough to get two bad breaks piled on like this—and that bad breaks is no pun!"

CHAPTER TEN

World Series Opening Game

Somehow Stub Alison felt a lot different as he warmed up Pete Ryder before the opening game of the World Series. This year the classic opened in the city of the Rebels, perennial pennant winners in their league. Rebel Stadium, one of the largest major-league parks capacity wise, was jammed and packed to the steel girders that supported the roof. More than seventy thousand fans overflowed the permanent seats.

Man, this was really something!

Stub realized fully the responsibility that rested on him, a rookie with scarcely half a season of big-league experience. He was filled with quiet determination to give Country Selder every last ounce of effort that he could summon. He recalled the manager's words while they went over and over the scouting reports on Rebel hitters.

"I'm going to tell you the same thing the manager of the

Goliaths told me going into my first World Series," Selder said. "I was a green rookie with barely a season of big-league play behind me. He told me to keep saying to myself that a World Series was just another set of ball games dressed up in fancy trimmings. Just play the best baseball you can. You hear, kid?"

Stub caught a pitch from Ryder and the big right-hander signaled that was enough. Stub looked around.

Bunting and flags draped the stands everywhere. Four bands blared from different vantage points. The governor of the state was prominent in a box near the Rebel dugout. He was laughing, holding court with other VIP's before time to throw out the first ball.

The rookie sucked in a breath. Just another series of ball games, Selder said. Oh, sure! The bases were ninety feet apart; the pitching rubber was sixty feet and six inches from the plate. A batter was allowed three strikes; the pitcher could not throw more than three times out of the strike zone without putting a batter on first base. The rules did not change for the World Series, but Selder was wrong.

A World Series game was not just another ball game. The big series was something special. It was a battle between the best clubs in baseball for the title World Champions. There was all the difference in the world.

Stub Alison was a chastened character. He had given very serious thought to a lot of things after Dahl's injury. There just was too much riding on every pitch of a World Series for anybody to risk tossing a wrench into a machine that had to mesh. Needling was out. Stub resolved firmly that he would cast no aspersion at anybody, no matter what.

The youngster's resolve was sorely tested in the very first inning of the opening game.

The star of the Rebel pitching staff, a cagey southpaw who had racked up twenty-three wins in the regular season, set down Fox, Samron, and Schmidt in order.

So what, Stub thought. If big Pete is right, he'll give Rebel hitters as rough a time as that wrong hander can give us.

The Rebel leadoff batter cut under Pete's high, hard one. A towering popup bored into the air, foul along the first-base line. Ark Molton charged in for it.

"Mine! Mine!" Molton shouted. "I've got it!"

Stub had flipped off his mask and started to be under the ball. Suddenly he saw that wind currents above the stands were driving the popup back toward the plate. The catch would be easier for him than for Molton.

"I'll take it!" The rookie catcher yelled. "Stay clear, Molton, stay clear!"

"Ark! Ark!" Pete Ryder yelled from the mound. "Take it, Ark!"

Now, Country Selder had a strict rule that a third man called the play in a situation of this kind. Alison obediently swerved out of Molton's path. Big Ark was just not quite agile enough. He made a frantic stab but the fast-descending ball barely ticked his mitt. It fell to the ground almost at the stocky catcher's feet.

Bitter, biting words rushed to Stub's tongue. He bit them back. Ark should have known more about the wind than to have called for that play. But it was Ryder who had called the play, probably expressing his lack of complete confidence in a rookie catcher. This was no time to shaft a barb at Molton.

"Tough," Stub said. He patted the big veteran on the shoulder. "Nice try. Doesn't mean a thing. We'll get him out of there!"

Molton gave the youngster an amazed stare. It was plain that he had expected Stub to blast him. Instead, the rookie had commiserated with him, condoned the error.

It happens so often that such a bobble proves costly that it is almost accepted as a baseball axiom. The batter, given another chance, lined a clean hit to left. Pete Ryder lost the second batter in trying to keep his pitches tough to bunt. Then both base runners were pushed along by a perfect sacrifice bunt.

Selder ordered Ryder to walk the batter intentionally to fill the empty base at first. That early in the game it was a gambling strategy, but Selder had faith in Ryder's ability to keep the pitches low and force batters to hit on the ground. A double play would pull the Goliaths out of the inning.

Ryder kept the pitches low. The Rebel batter rapped a skipping grounder a little to the left of second base.

Fox fielded the ball without error, but he had been a step slow in starting after it. He had to make a last second lunging grab. He was off-balance and the necessary fraction of a second required to steady himself for the toss to Banyan was costly. They had the runner at second. Banyan put all he had behind his throw to Molton. It was not enough. The ball hit the first baseman's mitt an instant after the Rebel runner's spikes bit into the first-base sack.

The runner who had been on third scored. Molton's quick peg to Alison was in plenty of time to head off the runner who had been on second. Stub efficiently blocked the base and put the tag on the Rebel crashing in. He clung to the horsehide although he was knocked sprawling.

A week ago a caustic observation from the rookie would have peeled Fox. The shortstop seemed to expect a jab. He threw a puzzled look at the rookie when Stub uttered not a word.

That lone Rebel run on the scoreboard loomed bigger and bigger. Inning after inning passed with the crafty Rebel southpaw in comfortable control of Goliath batters. Big Pete Ryder kept the Rebel attack equally well contained. Power hitters of both teams remained impotent against the superb pitching. But in the top of the ninth the Goliaths produced a golden opportunity to salvage the game.

Stub Alison led off. He went to bat filled with determination. He was oh-for-three. He didn't intend to let this southpaw hang the oh-for-four horse collar on him. He waited grimly for a pitch to his liking while the Rebel ace worked on him.

Letter high along the outside edge of the plate, but definitely outside. Ball one. A slider that eased away shoulder high and looked outside to Stub nicked the corner of the plate. Strike. One and one. A ball too low. Another ball, wide. A curve broken off sharp just above the knees and the count was full, the inevitable three and two.

Good hitters relish the three-and-two situation. Stub Alison was confident. He'll come in with that sinking curve, the rookie thought. Probably try to keep it on the outside.

He watched the ball closely. Sometimes you could see from the spin in time to know it was a curve. Not with this cagey leftie. He hid his pitch to the last instant and the ball was delivered in exactly the same manner as his other pitches.

The ball was a grayish-white streak speeding toward the plate. It was a mean pitch, aimed at the small area just above the knee and inside. It was the toughest kind of pitch for Stub to hit. The Rebels had scouting reports on Goliath hitters, too.

Stub gauged the pitch as maybe a fraction inside. But suppose it broke over the plate at the last second? Stub had started his swing when he saw that the ball was breaking in not outward.

He leaped and flung himself away from the plate. He just was not quick enough. The speeding ball cracked him above the right knee. Stub picked himself out of the dirt and jogged down the line to first base. He disregarded the dull throb of pain in his knee.

Play to win on the road and tie at home. The old baseball axiom. Banyan was at the plate. Banyan was a good hit-and-run man. Stub caught the hit sign that Selder passed to Banyan. Banyan stepped out of the batter's box, rubbed dirt on his hands, knocked his bat against the heel of his left spikes, then against the heel of the right spikes. That was Banyan's sign to the base runner that he would go after the second pitch.

The Rebel defense suspected a bunt. First baseman and third baseman charged in with the pitcher's delivery. The second baseman started for first to cover the bag. The pitch was high and tight, a tough pitch to bunt well. Banyan added to the Rebel belief by bluffing a bunt.

Stub got a good jump on the next pitch. The shortstop dashed to cover second because the second baseman was leaning a step toward first, again preparing to cover the bag on a bunt. Fox picked the right spot. He drilled the ball through the hole left at short.

Stub's stride was awkward. He saw Country Selder waving him to come on. But he knew that if he tried for third the play would be very close, that he would likely be thrown out. He knew that his speed was cut down by the pain in his knee. He half stumbled rounding second, stopped, and returned to the bag.

DeMino or Dahl would have been next at bat had either been playing. Selder had refused to disturb the batting order that had won the pennant. He had put Layne in the position the catchers had batted from. Now he passed the sacrifice sign to Layne.

Layne dumped two pitches—both foul. Then he swung too soon at a change-up pitch. A lazy fly bored into the sky. The Rebel left fielder camped under it. Stub would have been foolish to have attempted to advance on the short fly.

His knee throbbed with pain. He wondered if he imagined that it was stiffening. He saw Selder call to the dugout and a right-hand swinger came out to bat for Ryder. Stub prayed that the pinch hitter would get hold of a long one. He was not sure that he could score on a hit if it was only a single.

The pinch hitter swung mightily, but the Rebel pitcher had fooled him badly. The pitch was a slow, sinking curve. The batter topped the ball. It dribbled across the turf halfway between the mound and third base. Stub ran with all the speed he owned.

The pitcher juggled the ball momentarily and lost his chance to throw to second to go for a double play. Being a leftie, he had to pivot to throw. It was a shorter throw to third. He buzzed the ball that way and hard.

Selder signaled frantically for Stub to hit the dirt. The rookie flung his body forward in an all-out slide. The pitcher's hard throw was low. The ball cracked Stub squarely on the spot where he had been hit before, took a weird bound into left field. The Rebel shortstop and left fielder raced for the ball.

"Go on, kid, go on! You can beat the throw!"

Country Selder shouted. Stub scrambled to his feet. He tore for the plate. But the injured knee buckled. He stumbled and sprawled headlong in the dirt. He managed to struggle to his feet again, but the throw from left field smacked into the catcher's mitt while Stub hobbled ten feet from the plate.

Fox flied deep to left field for the final out and the game was over. Rebels, 1; Goliaths, 0. The hated champions of the other league had the important first-game win. It is a big edge in a short series.

Stub was overwhelmed in the dressing room.

"You run bases like a sandlotter. You should have been on third on Monk's smash through short!"

"Anybody inform you that this is the World Series, Rook!"

"And you're the noisy so-and-so who yelled at me all season about being slow and awkward!" Ark Molton snarled. "I never yet fell over my own feet and lost the run that would have tied a ball game!"

Stub seethed beneath the verbal blistering. He sat before his locker and gingerly pulled his pants over the bruised knee and tried to choke down the angry resentment that welled in him.

Did these crusty old buzzards think a fellow was made of steel? Two cracks from baseballs thrown as hard as that southpaw could heave them would slow up any of the veterans, that was for sure! They must have seen the ball hit him.

But Stub Alison made no comment aloud.

These guys had shown the league in the stretch drive that they were rough and tough. They had asked for no quarter nor given any. They would have no use for an Alibi Ike. Besides, if he whined about the knee, Selder might refuse to use him behind the plate tomorrow. With old Pete in there, things might be worse than having a fellow practically hobbling on one leg.

A good soaking in hot water and maybe a heat pad around the knee tonight and he'd be as good as new tomorrow.

CHAPTER ELEVEN

Series Goat?

The Goliath dressing quarters was a grim and silent place before the start of the second World Series game. Players sat on the benches before the row of lockers on the inside wall. Most of them stared at the floor. Gazes of a few followed Country Selder as he paced back and forth, slapping a rolled newspaper against his thigh. Selder's rugged features were set in hard lines that made his face appear more craggy than ever. His gray eyes held a steely hardness. He faced his men.

"I don't know how many nor which of you are responsible," Selder said. "It could be that none of you did such a foolhardy thing. Whatever the score is, I tell you that it is no good for the club and it had better not happen again!"

Selder unrolled the newspaper. Every man in the room had already seen the black headline that stretched across the paper.

GOLIATHS HURT BY ROOKIE'S
LACK OF EXPERIENCE

"That isn't true," Selder said. "It is understandable. This is not!"

The manager indicated the subhead beneath the headline. "Would have won with Dahl or DeMino behind the plate," say Goliath veterans.

"Milt Binkley says the character who wrote this thing is noted for being careless with the truth. He has been known not only to misquote but to make up items from thin air and attribute them to some sports figure. I hope such is the case in this matter. Mark this down, all of you: any information for sports writers from the Goliaths during the rest of the Series will be given out by me, or cleared through me.

"All right. We've gone over the Rebel batting order. We're shooting with Byrnes today. I don't have to tell you that this ball game is a must for us. Win today and go back to our own ball yard even up and we have the edge. Lose and go home two down and the Rebels have a tremendous bulge. I want to see Alison a minute. Everybody else out on the diamond."

Selder waited until the last of the other players had crowded out the doorway. He eyed the stocky rookie.

"How does the knee feel, kid?" Selder asked.

Stub jerked a quick gaze to the manager. "How did you know anything was wrong with my knee?"

"I'm not blind, kid. I saw that low inside pitch tag you yesterday. And the throw to third hit you about in the same spot. I'm an old-timer, kid, and I go along with the tradition that ballplayers shake it off when a pitch plunks them. I know all about the 'scrap iron' stuff about catchers, too. I tried to get in touch with your room last night. Where were you?"

"I never left the room. I was in the bathroom, soaking the knee in hot water and Epsom salts and the phone stopped ringing before I got to it. Anyway, the knee is fine. I had an electric pad on it all night, too."

Selder nodded. "Just to make sure," he said, "we'll have Doc take a look."

"It's all right," Stub protested. "I don't feel a twinge."

"Doc!" Selder called. A bald head poked around the corner of a little room partitioned off in the dressing quarters. "Give a look-see at the kid's knee," Selder said.

"Doc" was not short for Doctor in the case of the little bald man. But nobody ever called him anything else. He had been a fixture with the club for more than twenty years. Doc motioned for Stub to get up on a flat table. Doc's fingers probed gently around the knee. Stub did not flinch.

"See?" he said to Selder. "I told you it's all better."

"There's a little knottiness," Doc said. "But it does 'pear okay otherwise, Country. A rub with my special hot ointment will loosen it all the way."

"Get with it," Selder said. "If the kid isn't out there for infield workout, there's no telling what the press-box wolves will be sending out!"

"Yeah." Doc nodded. He reached in a bag and brought out a bottle, poured a gob of creamy-looking stuff in his palm and slapped it on Stub's knee. "It'll only take a minute," Doc said. "We'll take the Rebs today, huh, Country? That's if Lefty has his stuff. Does he come up with a lousy day like sometimes, they'll kill us!"

A few minutes later the area around his knee feeling warm and good, Stub recalled Doc's words. He had a feeling that this might be a "lousy day like sometimes" for Byrnes. It was kind of funny. Lefty's curve snapped off sharply. His fast ball smacked into the mitt with satisfying authority. And yet Stub had that feeling.

He had heard catchers with a lot more experience talk about a kind of sixth sense backstops developed. But they could be wrong, too. Stub hoped fervently that he was wrong about Byrnes this time.

Three Goliath batters went to the plate and contributed three routine outs in the top of the first. Stub became more and more leary about Byrnes as the southpaw worked on the Rebel leadoff man.

Lefty just was not right. In the parlance of ballplayers, he was "wild down the middle." His control was off just enough so that he missed the corners with his curve and went above or below the strike zone in moving his fast ball around. He was constantly behind the batter then would be forced to lay the ball in there. Rebel hitters lay back and waited and took toeholds on the cripple pitches.

Country Selder had pitchers heating up in the bullpen from the second Rebel batter. The Rebels notched three solid base hits in the first inning yet did not score.

The leadoff man singled sharply over third. He was one of the fastest men in the majors and led his league in stolen bases. Evidently the Rebel manager wanted to test Stub Alison's arm.

The speed merchant broke for second on Byrnes' third pitch to the next batter. Stub whistled a peg past Byrnes as though the ball had been shot from a rifle. Banyan had the ball in his glove and down in front of the bag as the runner started his slide. One out.

The batter set himself and lashed a fat pitch between Clancy and Samron. The ball banged against the facing of the lower right center stands. Only fast fielding and an accurate throw by Samron held the blow to a double.

The third batter tied into a curve that hung. He was a mite too far in front. Ark Molton barely had time to throw up his mitt. The ball would have been past him and into the right-field corner if he had needed to take one stride. As it was, Ark's snap throw after stabbing the drive almost doubled the runner off second.

Two out. Then the next batter lined a drive over second base.

Rog Samron raced in, saw that he could probably not make a shoestring catch, slowed a little. He was still moving forward when he grabbed the ball. His forward motion added momentum to his throw. Stub took the peg five feet down the third-base line.

The base runner was a big man. He hurled his bulk at the rookie catcher in more of a football block than a slide. Stub gave not an inch. He had the ball on the Rebel and clutched it tightly when they crashed together to the ground.

For three more innings luck and sensational fielding kept Rebel spikes from denting home plate. They put runners on base in every inning. They threatened all the time.

Perhaps if the Goliaths could have got Byrnes a one or two run margin, the left-hander might have worked out of his "wildness down the middle." But in four innings Goliath bats accounted for just two hits. Both were singles and in both instances double plays erased the base runners. In the bottom of the fourth two singles, a long double, and a triple to the flagpole in deep center field convinced Selder. Lefty Byrnes gave way for the Goliath middle-distance relief pitcher.

The reliever pitched to three batters and did not get one out. The bases had been cleared by a three-run homer when Tommy Cagni took over the mound duty. Cagni was a bonus pitcher the Goliaths had carried since signing him in June off a college campus. The ex-collegiate star gave solid evidence of developing into a big-league pitcher. In the heat of the torrid stretch drive, Selder had seldom pitched Cagni. Now, in the roughest of spots for a rookie pitcher to be shoved into, Cagni demonstrated that he owned pitching courage.

He blew down three Rebel hitters, simply overcame them with a blazing fast ball that was so much faster than they had been looking at that the Rebels could not time it. But a big 7 went on the scoreboard for the Rebels.

Experienced big-league pitchers ease off when they get a big lead, which probably explains why the Goliaths scored twice in the fifth. They might have made it a bigger inning except that Mike Clancy was caught on a cutoff play after socking a hit that he should have known better than to try to stretch.

Cagni retired the Rebels in order again in the bottom of the inning. There was no threat by the Goliaths in their sixth. Rebel hitters began to get Cagni's fire ball timed in their half of the sixth. He was hit hard but escaped run damage. Then in the home seventh the roof fell in on the young Goliath pitcher.

Cagni could not be handed all the blame. Listless, lackluster fielding—two errors of commission by Banyan and Fox and one of omission from Molton—turned the inning into a farce. Rebel hits combined with Goliath misplays for six more runs.

Through it all Stub Alison crouched behind the plate and uttered no word of condemnation aloud. He muttered several times but held back scorching words that formed ready to hurl at the veterans' misplays on the field.

Two more Rebel runs scored in the eighth. The enemy pitcher wasted no time in setting down the Goliaths in order in the top of the ninth and the Rebels raced into their clubhouse to pack, on the heavy end of the topheavy 15 to 2 score. Up in the press box Milt Binkley sat before his typewriter and scowled. He heard the discussion going on around him.

"Looks as though the alleged mighty Goliaths came down to their natural level today. . . . They're just not a solid ball club. It's hard to understand how they beat out the Hoppers! . . . You said it. How *did* they win a pennant? . . . They must have something! . . . If they have, it sure isn't showing!"

Finally one of the sports writers addressed a question to Milt Binkley. "What's with these guys of yours, Bink? Are they cracking up, getting ready to curl completely, and hand the Rebels a Series sweep?"

Milt Binkley looked up. He gave his hatbrim a slight shove with a thumb. He shrugged and spread his hands. "You tell me," he said. "They simply aren't the club that roared through the league the last month of the season."

"They don't have the old spark, Bink. Something seems to be missing."

"Yeah, something's missing, all right!" That was the writer who had by-lined the piece that ripped Stub Alison. "Jake Dahl and Tony DeMino," he went on. "A player who was with the Goliaths two years ago when they took the Rebels put it in so many words: Alison doesn't have what it takes to catch major-league ball. He's strictly a clown, a busher. He doesn't know how to handle his pitchers. And look at the way he blew that popup yesterday! Right in his pocket and he blows it and it leads to the only run of the ball game!

"For my money, Alison is already the Series goat—and the chances are his whiskers will get longer while the Rebs take the Series melon in four heats!"

CHAPTER TWELVE

Deep Trouble

The chartered plane that carried the Goliaths from the city of the Rebels was almost like a morgue. No one had much to say.

Stub Alison kept strictly to himself. He felt the gloom of his teammates keenly. Not that he was any degree happy himself. If only they would let down the bars a little. Couldn't they understand that all of the gab he had put out was—was—well, doggone it, a fellow just couldn't let everyone throw it into him and not dish it back! They ought to know that all the time the main idea had been to win ball games.

He was young. He was full of the spirit of youth. It was difficult for a fellow still nearly three years away from voting age to settle into the rut of battle-weary veterans. In spite of the jabs he had taken, in spite of cracks the veterans had made, a rookie named Alison would leap eagerly at the slightest chance to be friendly with the hard-shell veterans.

"I ought to have my head examined!" Stub told himself on the plane. "Not one of those tough monkeys has let down the bars a teeny and they aren't going to. Okay, so they don't go for me and maybe never will. The thing that's important now is what made them come apart at the seams today! Is it all me? Would Selder have a better team with Pete Hagan behind the bat?"

This club was capable of playing a brand of ball that still could beat the Rebels. Two games behind was not insurmountable. How many times in late August and September had the club won four out of five games? Or four straight, for that matter. In one stretch in September, when the pressure was on the most, the Goliaths had won eleven straight, and on the road! From the Bucks, Redbirds, Savages, and Hoppers. Any of those clubs would stack up right along with the Rebels and not show short.

The Goliaths could take the Rebels, too!

A curious thought flicked across the back of the rookie's mind. When we were in the hot streak that won our pennant, Molton and his pals were on me all the time and I was handing it back. Maybe we'd play better ball if— But that was a crazy thought!

Wonder if Goliath fans had given up on them? Wonder if they would stay away from the stadium? It was for sure *that* wouldn't happen. The fans would be out there to peel the hides off the team if they went sour.

Fans jammed the stadium for the third Series game. And they yelled loyally for their favorites.

"You have to say that this is as good a baseball city as any in the country," Milt Binkley sounded off proudly in the press box. "The fans are still back of the club. They know the boys can come back and nail the Rebels to the wall!"

"It won't be the Rebels who get nailed to the wall!" That was the sports scribe who had castigated Stub Alison in his game accounts. "Anybody who seriously thinks the Rebels won't win two before your gang of clowns can win four has a noggin filled with sawdust! Why, we're a cinch to take it in not more than six games. I'd say the chances are excellent that we'll wrap it up here in your own back yard!"

Country Selder could have pitched Ryder. The big right-hander had worked before with only three days of rest. He was no longer a youngster, though, and Selder knew four days' rest would be better. He would never have admitted it, but the thought that he just might need big Pete as a last-hope stopper for the fourth game could have come to Selder.

He chose to go with Duke Hendricks on the rubber despite the rough manner that Rebel power had exploded against the left-hand slants of Byrnes.

Stub felt different about Kendrick than he had in warming up Byrnes. Kendrick was sharp. His curve snapped off, his fast ball was alive. Best of all, he had pinpoint control when Stub moved the mitt target around.

Duke Kendrick proved that day that he also had his full share of pitching courage.

A less stout-hearted hurler would surely have thrown in the sponge and quit cold at the terrible support given

Kendrick in the field. Duke Kendrick hung in there and pitched over holes that shoddy fielding dug for him. Goliath bats remained in the strange deepfreeze that had thoroughly chilled the attack since the Series started. They gave Kendrick no margin at all to work under. Still the lean left-hander turned back Rebel hitters with a lion-hearted tenacity.

"Man, you're pitching!" Stub chunked the southpaw in the ribs as they entered the dugout after the top of the third. "I mean *really* pitching!"

A glaring error by Monk Banyan, a slow pickup of a bunt by Ark Molton that the official scorer ruled a hit but which should have been an out, another bad boot of a double-play ball by Fox had filled the bases with nobody out. Duke Kendrick stood out there and fired his fast ball and fanned two batters. Then he had caught a third batter with a deceptive change-up that was rolled back to the box.

"Let's get the Duke some runs!" Stub chirped in the dugout. "A fellow pitches an inning like he did ought to have a dozen runs handed him!"

The Goliaths went down in order.

For nine thrill-packed innings Duke Kendrick held off the relentless Rebel attack. In only one inning did the Rebels fail to get men on the bases. They had scoring opportunity after scoring opportunity. Duke Kendrick simply rose up in his pitching might and blew down the threats. The Duke was mighty tough in the pinches.

Stub kept the southpaw moving the ball around. He called the pitches according to the book that scouts had gathered on Rebel hitters and Kendrick's control was sharp enough to hit most of the mitt targets. They outguessed power hitters, fed them slow, teasing stuff when they were set for fast balls. They broke off curves and fast ones in tight when the Rebels crowded in and started swinging for the fences on the slow stuff.

The rookie catcher kept a running fire of chatter going. "Way to fire that rock, Left! . . . Slam it down Main Street this time! . . . Keep firing in there, Duke-boy! . . . What'd'ya say out there? The old pepper! . . ."

Always encouragement. Never a sarcastic peep at the bumbling play of the veterans.

It seemed as though Kendrick's great hurling was going to be wasted. The Rebels were famed in the sports sheets for their power at the plate, but all baseball men knew that the hard core of their success was a near-airtight defense and great pitching. Both departments were functioning perfectly this day.

Molton and Clancy and Schmidt and Samron and Alison did not go to the plate and rest their bats on their shoulders. Rebel fielders came up with great stops, great catches in the outer gardens. Rebel pitching was as tough as Kendrick's when Goliaths got on base.

An unbroken line of zeroes adorned the scoreboard for each team at the end of nine full innings. Kendrick blanked the Rebels in the top of the tenth. Stub Alison led off at the plate in the bottom of the inning.

The rookie worked the count to two-and-two. The fifth pitch was lower than he liked but he dared not risk taking it. He banged the low, outside pitch. The ball ripped down the third-base line, curving past the bag barely inside.

Banyan laid down a good sacrifice bunt to move the rookie to second. Stub yelled at Layne, "Just a little bingle! Just meet that apple!"

Layne lined to left. Stub did not try to advance after the catch. Duke Kendrick swung from his heels—and rolled weakly to the first baseman.

"Hang tough on that rubber out there," Stub told the southpaw. "We're bound to get you a run pretty soon!"

In the Rebel half of the eleventh the Goliath defense again faltered. Fox half-bobbled a roller to short and the batter got the decision at first base. Kendrick worked hard on the next man. Stub called for pitches toughest to bunt. They got a count of two-and-two on the batter. Then the Rebel caught the Goliaths with their defenses down.

He used his third strike to bunt. He laid a good, squirming bunt a foot inside the base path down the first-base line. Molton ambled in, grabbed the ball, and threw hurriedly to Banyan covering first base. His hurried throw drew Banyan off the bag and the runner was safe.

Schmidt must have seen the batter drop his bat for a bunt at the last instant. The Goliath third baseman had raced in. Fox should have slanted over to cover third but he had not done so. The Rebel runner from first base saw that the base was unguarded. Banyan had to hold up a throw from first base until Fox ran belatedly to cover. The runner did not even need to slide. A man on third and a man on first now and nobody out.

"Don't mind it, Duke!" Stub yelled at his pitcher. "You can pitch over it. Only three to get, Duke—only three."

The words were barely out before Stub knew he should

never have yelled them. Duke Kendricks owned more superstitions than usual. One of the strongest was that it was fatal for a teammate to remind a pitcher how many men he needed to retire. It would have been all right to have shouted a general warning that nobody was out. But it was a sure jinx to yell to a pitcher that he had only two, or one, or three to get out.

Duke's next pitch was high, wide, and handsome. Stub had to leap to knock down the near-wild pitch. The runner on first scurried down to second. Molton came down the line and called for the ball. Stub threw it to him.

"That finishes us," Molton spat. "You put the whammy on the Duke right!"

Duke Kendrick made an effort to calm down. He laid the next pitch squarely down the middle. The batter leaped at it. His bat cut viciously. He was overanxious to kill that fat pitch.

Stub recognized the squashy sound that bat and ball made. He jerked off his mask. He located the undercut popup. He raced back and toward the Rebel dugout back of third base. The ball was coming down close to the field boxes beyond the dugout but it was not going to be out of reach. Stub saw Schmidt lumbering toward the ball.

"I'll take it!" Stub yelled.

He motioned Schmidt back. He was under the ball drifting toward the stands.

"Ya-ah-h!" A strident shout came from the Rebel dugout. "Look out for the rail! LOOK OUT FOR THE RAIL!"

Stub grinned. How many times had they yelled things

like that at each other in kid games? Look out for the bicycle! Look out for the bats! You wouldn't think big leaguers would yell like kids.

Anyway, they had a fine chance to rattle him out of *this* catch. The infield could lay back for two after this putout. Duke would keep the pitches low, try to force the batter to hit on the ground. They might get a double play that would end the inning without—

An abrupt and terrifying possibility popped into the rookie's thoughts. Suppose no one was covering the plate! Base runners were entitled to advance on caught fouls, if they could make it.

Stub took his gaze off the ball an instant. The umpire had followed Stub to watch that he made the catch fairly. The Rebel batter was the only man near the plate. The man on third was tagged up and ready to dash for the unguarded plate.

Stub swiveled his gaze back, found the ball. He slapped his mitt against the horsehide, knocked it high into the stands so there could be no question that it was *not* caught.

Duke Kendrick did not get another strike near the plate. Country Selder walked out to the mound to talk to the southpaw as the batter trotted to first with a base on balls. Stub walked down pitcher's lane.

"Come on, Duke," he said. "Settle down. You can't hand them the game on a platter!"

"No, you can't do that, Duke!" Ark Molton had come over from his position. He snorted and glared at Stub. "*You've* already done that!"

"Knock it off!" Country Selder gave Molton a brief

look. The manager asked Stub a question. "Has Kendrick lost his stuff?"

"Huh-uh." The rookie shook his head. "He's still got good stuff. He can get these fellows out!"

"Okay, you pitch to one more man, Kendrick!"

Kendrick walked the batter. The first run of the game was forced across the plate. Selder came out and took the ball from the southpaw. A relief pitcher came through the bullpen gate out in right field.

A Rebel long-ball hitter picked on the reliever's first pitch. The drive was a home run all the way. After that long swat the relief pitcher closed the door, retired three men in a row. But the damage was done. It would have been difficult to have found anyone in the stadium who thought other than that the Goliaths were whipped.

In the dugout Stub Alison unfastened his shin guards and protector. He heaved them into the corner in disgust. Rog Samron was leading off. But from the general attitude in the dugout the impression that three batters would go to the plate, go through the motions, and retire to the showers was strong.

"Get on, Rog!" Stub did not realize that he barked the words. "Let's show the world there are at least a couple of the great Goliaths who haven't rolled over to play dead yet!"

"Play dead!" Monk Banyan exploded. "Who's the guy that murdered us, tell me that!"

"Yeah." Fox threw in his nickel's worth. "You're the sawed-off palooka who killed any chance we had to get back in the Series!"

Stub stared first at Banyan then at Fox. Red flamed beneath the rookie's tan. This was just too much.

"*I* killed any chance to— Why, you triple-distilled jugheads! If I had caught that foul, a run would have scored. If you thick-skulled has-beens had brains enough to keep your ears apart you'd know there was nobody covering the plate!"

The rookie's jaw stuck out. He eyed the veterans.

"Okay, so the guy got on base. Who put out crummy fielding all day that sandlotters would be ashamed of!"

Bitter resentment overflowed in Stub. He had laid off these crusty veterans because he was anxious to do anything to help the team win. But who was cracking up under pressure? It wasn't Samron or Cagni or Layne or Alison, the young players on the club. His blue eyes blazed as the youngster let loose on the veterans.

"If your brain worked anywhere near as quick as your tongue, you wouldn't have been outsmarted on that bunt," he shot at Molton.

Then he flamed at Fox.

"And if you had driven those spavined Charley horses of yours over to cover the bag, the other runner would have been held at second!"

Ark Molton opened his mouth as though he was going to say something. Stub whirled on him.

"Don't say it, you blubber-laden whale! Your waistline isn't the only fat about you. The lard has gone to your head until you don't have gumption enough to cover home when your rotten support has made a pitcher too weak to take it himself!"

Stub glared at the veterans again.

"Oh, there's no doubt that I lost the game! It wouldn't be lost yet to a real ball club. You still have a time at bat but you've given up already. The rough, tough, battling Goliaths—hah! You can have them!"

Not a word was made in reply to the rookie. The umpire called, "Batter up! Get somebody out here!"

Rog Samron made the pitcher come in there with his pitches. He refused to bite at teasers just out of the strike zone. Samron drew a walk.

"All right, all right!" Country Selder yelled in the third-base coaching box, and clapped his hands. "Keep it going, Schmidt! It's never too late for a rally!"

Schmidt lined the third pitch into left field, a clean single. Samron stopped at second.

"The merry-go-round, the merry-go-round!" Selder yelled. "Grab the brass ring for a free ride, Mike, grab the brass ring!"

The Rebels knew there would be no bunt. Their infield played deep. Outfielders were almost to the warning track around the outfield. The Rebels respected Big Mike's power.

Clancy really belted a fast ball. The horsehide rode high and far. It seemed as though it was surely in the left-center stands. The left fielder raced at top speed. He timed his leap perfectly and stretched gloved hand as high as possible. The ball stuck in the leather and the fielder hung onto it despite crashing into the wall and tumbling to the ground. The ball had been hit deep enough so that Samron scooted to third and Schmidt lumbered to second after the catch.

With one out, the Rebels played for the man at the plate. They ignored the base runners. These runs meant nothing. The Rebels would gladly trade a run for an out at this point. They pitched Molton low.

Everybody knew the big fellow was very slow afoot. Any ground ball that an infielder could reach would almost surely be an out.

Big Ark did not hit on the ground.

His long bat whipped around much like a golfer whips his driver. He golfed a low, fast one that certainly was faster when it left the bat. The ball landed high against the fence in deep center field beyond the flagpole, the farthest point from home plate in Goliath Stadium. It would have been a home run inside the park for a man with any speed. Ark Molton puffed into third as the outfield relay was taken in short left by the shortstop.

Two runs in. Man on third. Stub Alison at the plate. Abruptly there was feverish activity in the Rebel bullpen. Molton growled something to Country Selder, then Ark Molton yelled at Stub.

"Time to back up some of that fighting talk, Rook! You'd better bust one!"

Stub Alison drilled a sizzling drive between first and second. The second baseman dived all out but failed to touch the ball. Molton scored, of course. The throw in went to second base.

Rebels, 5; Goliaths, 3.

The tying run was at the plate. One out. The Goliaths were abruptly very much back in the ball game. The Rebel manager came from the dugout. He held conference with his catcher and pitcher at the mound. He took the ball from the pitcher and motioned toward the bullpen. It was a right-hander who came through the bullpen gate.

The relief pitcher threw one ball. It was a curve on the inside.

Layne hit the ball a mile a minute—in one skittering hop into the third baseman's glove. Quick throw to the second baseman, kick the bag and sidestep while Stub was twenty feet from the base, easy throw to first. Double play. End of game. End of Goliath threat.

Rebels, 5; Goliaths, 3.

The Goliaths were no longer in the game.

Rebels three games won; Goliaths no game won.

The Goliaths were barely in the Series!

CHAPTER THIRTEEN

Astounding Order

Stub Alison bolted his dinner, grabbed an armful of newspapers in the hotel lobby, and hurried to his room. He was glad that he had turned down Duke Kendrick's proposition to share an apartment after he rejoined the Goliaths. He was glad that he had a room to himself. He doubted that he could stand any of the Goliaths tonight. The sports sheets added nothing to his ease of mind.

It was to be expected that the death knell of the Goliaths would be sounded. But the general tone of the writeups badly shook up the rookie.

ROOKIE CATCHER FAILS GOLIATHS AGAIN! . . . LISTLESS PLAY IN FIELD SPEARHEADED BY GOLIATH RECEIVER! . . . COUNTRY SELDER DESPERATE SEARCHING END OF SLUMP AT PLATE—AND BEHIND PLATE!

Those were some of the headings of sports-sheet stories. Only the *Gazette* did not, at least, hint that the Goliath collapse was directly traceable to Stub Alison. Stub read Milt Binkley's piece a second time.

"*This corner holds stubborn belief that the cause of our Goliaths is not entirely without hope. True it is that we are unable to unearth evidence in the record book that any club ever came back to win the Series after dropping three games behind, especially three games to none. But nothing was ever in a record book until somebody did something never done before. Now is certainly a time for the Goliaths to put themselves permanently in the record books.*

"*There are signs that the club may be pulling out of the dismal batting slump that has held a vise grip the first three games. Throw out the second game as one of those nightmares that happen to any club, and the Rebels have not manhandled Goliath pitching. We believe that Ryder can beat the Rebs. Kendrick showed today that Rebel power does not scare him, and we hold that Lefty Byrnes could come back. But most of all, the Goliath uprising in their last at bats today is indication that they may be coming alive.*

"*We believe that the Goliaths will be the club they were in mid-September for the rest of the Series. We are going out on the proverbial limb and predicting that the Series will go the full seven games and that the game count will then be Goliaths 4 and Rebels 3.*"

Stub read the syndicated column by-lined by the writer who had ripped him before. The same treatment was here.

"Your correspondent has been consulting the record books on World Series boo-boos. There was the $30,000 muff that Fred Snodgrass made in 1912, and the foul pop that Fred Merkle let drop at his feet to give Tris Speaker opportunity to deliver the winning base hit in the final game of the same Series. A young Phil Cavaretta cut off an outfield throw that allowed Mickey Cochrane to score the winning run of the 1935 Series.

"Carl Hubbell pitched a home-run ball to Lou Gehrig to lose the 1936 Subway Series between the Yankees and the Old Giants. There have been other boo-boos of note. All of them pale into insignificance compared with the classics that Alison is compiling for the Goliaths.

"His inexcusable failure to smother a measly pop foul today was worse even than the rock he pulled on another popup in the first game. Goliath veterans put it mildly in telling us that Alison is hurting them— Alison has killed them!

"Duke Kendrick deserved a better fate, as did Ryder earlier. It is tragic when well-pitched games go down the drain because a callow rookie can't deliver when the pressure is on. . . .

Gloom held Stub Alison. Maybe it *was* him. All the writers couldn't be wrong. Oh, sure, Milt Binkley didn't go along, but Binkley was a pal of Selder and—

A knock on the door interrupted the youngster's thoughts. "Come on in," he called. "It's not locked."

The last person the rookie expected—or wanted to see —opened the door. Ark Molton gave Stub an uncertain look.

"I guess I'm early, or something, kid," Molton said. "Maybe I'd better wait in the— But that wouldn't look so good, either."

Molton came into the room and closed the door. It wasn't until an hour or so later that the fact registered with Stub that Molton had said "kid" instead of "rook" or "busher." Right at the moment Stub was thinking of but one thing: this big ape had a crust coming to his room! He said shortly, "What do you want?"

"Now, wait a second, kid. Climb down off your war horse and—"

"This is my room," Stub interrupted. "I certainly did not invite you to visit me. If you came here to—to—well, if you have anything to say, say it and get out! Or have you already said everything to your sports-writer stooge!"

"Now, wait a second," Molton repeated himself. "You've got things all wrong. I didn't open my peep to that writing guy nor anybody else. I don't believe any of the rest did, either. You've got no license to get up on your ear!"

"Hah!" Stub snorted. His face flamed from the anger he tried hard to contain. Suddenly it seemed that a dam that held back pent-up emotion broke. He clenched his fists and took a step toward Molton.

"Get out, I tell you! Get out before I throw you out!"

It would have been funny to an observer. Ark Molton stood just over six-four and weighed two-twenty. Stub Alison was a scant five-seven and tipped the scales at a bare one hundred and sixty-five. But Ark Molton backed a step in the face of the blazing intensity of the youngster.

"Why, danged if you don't mean it!" Respect came into Molton's eyes. "You fighting little rooster! Hold it, you're no match for me, kid!"

Ark Molton threw brawny arms around Stub's shoulders, momentarily pinning his arms down. Stub wrestled to free himself. The door opened. Milt Binkley and Country Selder stood in the doorway. The manager looked swiftly at his players.

"What goes on here?" Selder's tone was oddly flat.

A silence held for a long moment. Ark Molton loosened his bear-hug grip. He looked at Binkley, then at his manager. The big man squirmed uneasily.

"Why, it's like this, Country," he began lamely. "I came up here to— That is, Binkley said he'd be here and we'd—like I said, I came up here to—"

"—Sort of talk over ways and means of winning tomorrow," Stub cut in.

Selder grunted. "It sounded like it from the hall," he said. "You were maybe rehearsing ways to maim Rebel pitchers and waylay their hitters?"

Nobody said anything for a moment. Finally Selder said in that soft drawl: "Let it go. I don't go for whiners—but I don't go for monkeys on my ball club brawling among themselves, either. You can take off, Molton."

"I explained to Country, Ark," Binkley said. "He just

about blew me down before I could convince him that I did not approach the kid directly, that it was strictly between you and me. The way it is, Country wants it handled between him and Alison from here on."

"You're not to breathe a word to anybody," Selder said. He eyed the burly first baseman. "And I mean not to *anybody!* You hear?"

Ark Molton nodded. He said, "There won't be any leak from me. I haven't let on to any of the others, have I?"

Molton left. Stub Alison looked from Binkley to Country Selder and back again. Bewilderment filled his blue eyes.

"I don't get any part of this," Stub said. "What was handled strictly between you and Molton?" He turned to Selder. "What's going to be handled from here on strictly between you and me?"

"You tell him, Bink," Selder said. "I have a feeling that if I rehash the thing too much I'll call it all off!"

"There's not much to it, kid," the sports writer said. "I don't suppose it ever entered your head. I'll give it to you like I gave it to convince Country.

"When you came with the Goliaths, you got off to a needling spree with Molton, Clancy, Banyan—let's just say the veteran players on the club. Nobody noticed at the time, but I've checked since. The club played sharper, better ball while the rhubarb went on. Sully shipped you down to the Dees and the club collapsed. Selder took over. The team spruced up but were still ninety miles from acting like a pennant contender. We really began to be a contender the day Country stuck you in left field—and the battle of verbal barbs between you and the vets began again. The Goliaths became the hottest team in the major leagues."

Binkley stopped a moment.

"I suggested to Country that the needling you gave the oldsters was responsible," he went on. "I wanted him to let me talk to you about continuing. He blew a fuse, but he didn't forbid me to talk to Molton. Probably didn't think of it. Anyway, I laid the cards on the table for Molton. You can say that the big fellow is past his peak, but don't ever think Ark Molton isn't a true pro. Winning means most to Ark. He not only wants the prestige that goes with a winner, but he wants the extra money. Ark agreed to goad you into resuming the needling rhubarb—and we won the pennant."

Again Binkley stopped speaking a moment. He looked a little thoughtful. He went on then.

"I suppose you probably made a vow to yourself not to bite back. You weren't going to do anything to jeopardize the chances of the team in the World Series. What you thought doesn't matter. What does matter is that the ball club just hasn't been the real Goliaths until today. You blew up and dished out the barbs and suddenly the team resembled the battling, clawing outfit that trampled Savages and Hoppers into the ground!"

Stub Alison just looked at the sports writer when Binkley finally stopped speaking altogether. His blue eyes held bewilderment still when the youngster shifted his gaze to Selder.

"It sounds as though he's saying in a kind of left-hand

way that it's good for the team for me to razz the veterans," he said. "That it is okay if I—if I—"

"—Open the gates and flood those guys with jabs," Binkley said. "Tell him it's all right, Country."

Country Selder drew in a long breath. He puffed out his cheeks and for an instant a frown held his craggy face. Then he let the breath out.

"It's not only okay if you do, kid," the manager said. "You're going to get aboard that crew early and often tomorrow. And the rest of the Series. That's an order, you hear!"

CHAPTER FOURTEEN

Champions Don't Stay Down

Country Selder called his team together in the clubhouse before the fourth game. His Georgia drawl did not exactly rasp but every man was aware that Selder meant every word he said.

"I'm not a college coach handing out a fight talk," he he said. "I'm a professional talking to a gang of pros. It seems advisable to call a few things to your attention. First of all, you are the champions of a major league. You whipped four good, tough ball clubs to gain that title and you're representing them and the whole league against the best the other league could produce!"

Selder stopped speaking for a full thirty seconds. His words bit when he did speak.

"SO FAR YOU HAVE LOOKED MORE LIKE THE CELLAR CHAMPIONS OF THE PODUNK-VILLE SANDLOT LEAGUE!"

The manager's glance drifted over the group.

"When I took this job," he said, "I went along with some of you in the face of strong criticism. I've always expected the best you have. That's all I'm asking now, but I want that! I tell you frankly, there will be a lot of you not wearing Goliath uniforms next year if you don't snap out of it. We can take the Rebels if we play heads-up ball. Get out there and play it! That's all!"

Selder sidled past his catcher as Stub warmed up Ryder in front of the stands behind first base.

"Don't forget your orders, kid. Get on them and stay on them!"

Stub nodded. At the moment the rookie catcher had another trouble on his mind. He was experiencing that odd feeling about Ryder. He put it out of his mind. He followed his manager's orders. Before two innings were complete he had the veterans on their toes in self-defense.

Ark Molton was thrown out on a close play after hitting to deep short in the first frame. Stub let him have it.

"Out of respect for feeble guys like you there should be a special allowance for you to use a wheel chair. Then if you slapped one against the wall, you might make it to first!"

Ark jerked a look at the rookie and Stub was sure that the eyelid away from him fluttered. Then Molton glared at the catcher and scowled and muttered something beneath his breath.

In the field, Mike Clancy ran a long way after a foul down the right field line. He didn't quite catch up to the ball. At the end of the inning Stub dragged an oilcan from beneath the dugout bench.

"Here, Alley Oop," he said. "This is a special dinosaur oil for time-worn joints. Maybe you'll be able to get off a dime out there if you use it!"

Suddenly the Goliaths were the fighting, snarling, aggressive team that had beaten down the challenge of good clubs in their own league. It was well that they were.

With a comfortable three-game margin, the Rebels were relaxed. Their manager could afford to gamble. He started a young pitcher on the mound who had plenty of stuff but was inclined to be wild. Goliath bats, combined with walks, chalked up four runs in the second inning.

It was a nice working margin for Ryder and normally more than he needed. The relaxed Rebels did not appear to be concerned. In the third they began taking the big Goliath right-hander apart. Selder signaled the bullpen into activity when Ryder walked a man to fill the bases. Still the manager was disinclined to jerk his pitcher.

Ryder could work out of the jam. But Ryder did not work out of the jam. Before a relief pitcher could put out the fire, six Rebels crossed the plate.

Then the fun began. The youngster on the mound for the Rebels had hit a long triple in the big inning. The base running did him no good. The Goliaths took *him* apart in their half of the inning.

Crash! Bang! Whiz!

Base hits rattled off Goliath bats. Two doubles, a single, a walk, and an error, then Ark Molton swaggered to the plate. Molton really tagged a fast ball. The drive cleared the left-field wall by twenty feet. Six runs went on the board for the Goliaths at inning end.

That game saw more pitchers stream from the bullpens than had the second game. The parade of runners crossing the plate was bigger than the constant stream of pitchers.

In the seventh inning the Goliaths were on the long end of a 13 to 8 count. Stub Alison banged one against the right-field barrier. The right-fielder played the rebound well. Stub was forced to slide hard into second. He felt his knee twinge. Gingerly he eased off the base.

Had he reinjured his knee?

Layne grounded out and the pitcher fanned. But Fox came through with a long hit. Stub loped easily around third and coasted home. He was thankful that he hadn't been forced to sprint. Fox reached third base.

Samron poked a single through the box and Fox raced home. In the dugout he growled at Stub.

"What's the idea blocking the paths, busher? I could have made it a homer inside the park if I hadn't had to slow down for you!"

Players on the bench took it up.

"He was taking a coffee break, that's all!"

"Guess who could use some of that special oil now!"

"The Skipper said to play heads-up ball. The rook played it so high he couldn't see he was running all in one place!"

The Rebels picked up a pair of counters in the eighth and the Goliaths came in for their bats, leading 15 to 11.

"The way this game's going, a four-run bulge could be wiped out quick like," Country Selder said. "Let's get some more!"

Schmidt led off. The fourth Rebel pitcher could not locate the plate and Schmidt walked. He moved to second on Clancy's sharp single. Schmidt advanced to third while the Rebels attempted a double play on Molton's sharp rap to short. Mike Clancy ruined the twin killing by bowling over the pivot man. Stub came to bat still seething from the scorching he'd got from the bench.

The pitcher tried to slip a fast ball past the youngster. Stub leaped at the pitch. He swung with every atom of power in his stocky frame.

Crash! Whi-z-z-z!

The ball left the bat like a rocket leaving the firing pad. Everybody in the park recognized that the smash was a home run even before it cleared the barrier in right center. But it never would have been surmised as an out-of-the-park homer by watching Stub Alison.

He tore down the first-base line like he was beating out a bunt. He rounded second, cutting the sack with his inside foot, and barreling toward third like a track man coming into the stretch. He steamed past third and a gaping Country Selder in the coaching box. He pumped for home with everything his short legs owned. He was right on the tail of Ark Molton approaching the plate. Ten feet from home, Stub launched a beautiful slide and crossed the rubber in a cloud of dust.

The Rebel catcher, the umpire, Monk Banyan—next batter—and Molton stared at the youngster as though they wondered if he had flipped completely. He strolled non-chalantly to the dugout. Molton stared at him fixedly. Fox just stared.

"Just what," said the shortstop, "was the big idea of *that* display?"

"Why, no idea at all," said Stub. "You remarked something about blocking the base paths. You frightened me, that's all, and I ran!"

Those three runs proved to be the winning margin. The Rebels counted four times and had two men on base in their ninth before the fifth Goliath pitcher finally induced a batter to rap a double-play ball.

Goliaths, 18; Rebels, 15.

The final figures on the scoreboard were more like a football score than a World Series. But Country Selder was satisfied. He had managed to get by with second-line and relief pitchers after Ryder departed. He had Byrnes and Kendrick ready. Ryder would be ready by the seventh game—if the Series lasted.

It had to last! This club was just finding itself.

Lefty Byrnes had plenty of rest for the fifth game. This time the Goliaths held him up in the field and they continued to maul Rebel pitching. Byrnes coasted in with a three-hit, 7 to 2 win in the final game at Goliath Stadium.

The real masterpiece of pitching for the entire Series came two days later in Rebel Stadium. Duke Kendricks came within one measly bingle that the Rebs got in the second of matching Don Larsen's famed Series perfect game. Duke did not feel bad.

"Beating those jokers would have been enough, shutting

them out on one hit is just mustard on the hot dog." Duke grinned as he made the remark in the dressing room, a soft drink in one hand and a hot dog in the other. "Boy," he chortled, "how I go for mustard on hot dogs!"

Sports writers ran out of superlatives in praising the Goliath comeback. They called it everything from an amazing reversal of form to a baseball miracle. They sought for some explanation of the club's about-face.

Milt Binkley knew, but he had pledged secrecy to Country Selder. It just might be that the magic would not work if the veterans got wise. The kid had lifted the club off the floor. It couldn't be in the cards now that the Rebels would get them down again.

CHAPTER FIFTEEN

Hot Bat

Country Selder pinned his hopes for the World Championship on Ryder. If the veteran right-hander was right, he would turn back the Rebels as he had in the opening game. If Ryder was sour, the Rebels would murder him.

Today Ryder was right. He got off to a shaky start and spotted the Rebels a two-run lead in the first inning. Stub, though, knew the right-hander was going to settle down. Ryder hit his real stride after the shaky start.

In the fourth, fifth, and sixth Ryder mowed down the Rebels in order. The two-base hit in the second was a Texas Leaguer that Fox just barely failed to reach in time. It and the walk Ryder gave up in the third did no damage. The Goliaths broke their string of zeroes on the scoreboard in the top of the sixth.

Holding the Goliaths hitless for five innings, the Rebel pitcher had been bearing down on every batter and he weakened. Ryder and Fox hit the ball hard—but straight at fielders. Rog Samron ripped a line drive down the left-field line good for two bases. Schmidt promptly drove a screamer between left and center and Samron scored without a play being made on him. Ark Molton loomed at the plate. The Rebel manager called a relief pitcher from the bullpen.

Ark Molton, slugger de luxe, looked toward the on-deck circle where Stub crouched. Molton seemed expectant. Stub did not fail him, but he waited until Molton had swung and missed, taken a wide ball, then swung and missed a sinking curve for two strikes. It looked as though the pitcher had Molton's number.

"Let it hit you, Sidepork," Stub yelled. "We need this run!"

Molton threw a peculiar glance over his shoulder at the rookie catcher. The next pitch was inside. Molton made a big deal of dodging it but Stub was watching closely and he was sure that Molton deliberately allowed the ball to plunk him in the ribs. The umpire motioned the big first baseman to take his base.

The Rebels protested vigorously. They claimed that Molton purposely stepped into the pitch. As usual, the decision of the umpire stood.

Stub did a lot of thinking while the rhubarb between umpire and Rebels went on. He recalled that this pitcher had fanned Molton three times in a previous appearance in the Series. The youngster stood outside the batter's box and looked down toward Molton. It took plenty of intestinal fortitude to stand up there and risk a broken rib in order to get on base. The least a fellow could do was to make it pay off.

The rookie hit the ball solidly. Unfortunately it was hit to a spot requiring the center fielder to move only five or six steps to his left to be in front of the drive.

Stub lowered his head as he passed Molton on the way to the dugout after his catching gear.

"Nice going, you old walrus," the rookie said. "I owe you an apology. That was something. I didn't really mean for you to get yourself beaned in order to get on base!"

"Button your lip!" Molton glowered. "It was strictly an accident!"

Stub looked up, saw that Monk Banyan was in earshot, and knew that Molton was protesting for the benefit of the second baseman. Banyan glared at the rookie.

Ryder's stuff lasted through the sixth but it was plain to Stub that the killing pressure was taking its toll. The Rebels put two men on base in that inning. Only a spectacular stop and throw by Fox from deep in the hole kept them from scoring.

In the seventh the Rebels increased the pressure on the veteran right-hander. Their best power hitter led off. He tied into Ryder's second pitch and belted a home run into the bleachers. A 1 to 1 deadlock now. Ryder escaped without further run damage but now the folks were as good as the people.

The eighth and ninth innings of that game provided the wildest, most thrill-packed play of the entire Series. Fans will replay it around the Hot-Stove league for many winters.

Ryder got himself into immediate trouble in the bottom of the eighth by handing out his second walk of the game to the first batter he faced. Country Selder phoned Pete Hagan to get every pitcher in the bullpen loose and ready.

The second batter ran the count to two-and-two. The big right-hander tried to sneak a curve past the hitter and the Rebel sliced it to right center for a clean hit. Fast fielding by Samron held the base runner from first from going to third.

Ryder walked the third batter in attempting to pitch so he could not bunt. Country Selder came from the dugout and took the ball from Ryder. He patted Ryder on the shoulder then signaled the bullpen with his left arm. There was a pause, then the public-address system blared.

"Your attention, please. Kendrick now pitching for the Goliaths—Kendrick!"

Duke Kendrick coming back after that beautifully pitched shutout yesterday!

Stub Alison carried the ball out to the mound after taking Kendrick's final range-finding pitch.

"There won't be any jinx cracks from me today," the stocky catcher said. "There won't be any missed popups. Pour that seed in to me, fellow!"

Duke Kendrick poured "that seed" in there. He brushed past the first man he faced with four pitches. The infield still played in on the grass. They could not afford to lay back and play for two with that big run on third.

Kendrick got two strikes on the batter, but on the next pitch Stub's heart jumped into his mouth. Seasoned ash met speeding horsehide with the sharp crack that denotes a ball hit squarely on the good wood of the bat. Stub didn't really see the ball streak off the bat. He only saw Ark Molton fling his massive body to his left and down. The big fellow came up with the ball and whistled a perfect throw to the plate.

Stub stood straddle of the base line a little to the third-base side. The ball smacked into his mitt. He whirled, braced to meet the runner barreling in from third—and dropped the ball!

Duke Kendrick blew three sizzling fast balls past the next batter. Then Rog Samron raced to the flagpole and snagged a drive to end the inning. But the run that went on the scoreboard for the Rebels was mighty, mighty big. Rebels, 2; Goliaths, 1.

Hot tears welled in Stub's eyes. A great lump swelled in his throat. What a time to drop a throw! He had no excuse. The peg from Molton had been arrow straight. He'd had the ball in plenty of time. All he had to do was put the tag on his man—and he'd muffed it!

Gloom was thick enough in the dugout to be cut. Never had Stub Alison been lower. At that moment he agreed with all the things that had been written about him in the sports sheets. He deserved anything his teammates might say to him.

Nobody made a peep for what seemed like an hour to the youngster. It was Monk Banyan who finally popped off.

"Seems to me," the second baseman began, "that we've taken a lot of stuff from a certain rook that—"

"Can it, Monk!" Ark Molton's tone was gruff. He threw a glance at Stub, then scowled at Banyan. "That's not the first error this club has made by a couple of million miles! We all know the kid would give his right arm to have it back. That one run won't win this ball game! Let's take it out on the Rebs instead of scrapping among ourselves!"

Stub Alison stared at the veteran first baseman. Molton scowled. "Keep on us, kid," he growled. "We're going to get 'em!"

Samron led off the Goliath ninth. The fleet outfielder swung hard at a sinker and topped the ball. A so-called swinging bunt dribbled down the third-base path. Samron's speed paid off. He turned the slow roller into a "leg hit" by beating the throw a hair.

Play for a tie at home and to win on the road. Would Country Selder follow the old axiom? This was the World Series, a little different from an ordinary game. Schmidt was a good bunter, notoriously a slow base runner. He could easily hit into a double play. Selder hung out the sacrifice sign.

The Rebels must have been figuring along the same lines as the Goliath manager. First baseman and third baseman charged in with the pitcher's delivery. Schmidt laid down a perfect sacrifice bunt, a twisting dribbler midway between third and the mound. The second or two required for the third baseman to veer in order to grab the ball ruined any chance of getting fleet-footed Samron at second.

Mike Clancy stalked to the plate. Ark Molton left the dugout for the on-deck circle. Stub sidled beside the first baseman.

"Thanks for going to bat for me," Stub muttered. "Get hold of one when you get up there, big man. Please! Get us in front!"

"Lay off that please stuff." Molton scowled again. "Get it through your nut that nothing's changed!"

The Rebel manager went out to the pitching mound. He and the catcher and the pitcher held a brief conference. When the first pitch came to Clancy, the Rebel strategy was apparent. They were filling the empty base. With slow-footed Molton coming up and the equally slow Clancy on first they would be almost sure of a double play on any grounder that could be reached.

"Bust one, Ark!"

"Pickle that onion, big fellow!"

Yells came from the dugout. Ark swung lustily and missed a down-breaking curve six inches. He fouled another pitch into the screen. Two pitches came in 'way too low. Ark fouled another, a weak roller down third-base way that almost rolled fair.

Stub hesitated. Then as Molton backed out of the batter's box and glanced his way it suddenly came to the rookie that Molton *wanted* the needle.

"Come on, Methuselah!" the rookie yelled shrilly. "Get a bat you can swing. You're too old and feeble to get a man-sized club around in time!"

It may not have been the crack and again it just might have been that Molton was kind of conditioned to respond to the rookie's jibes. Molton pulled an inside low pitch that went past the third baseman's dive as if it was jet propelled. The ball slanted off the facing of the left-field stands on the first long bound then bounced around in the corner. Samron scored. Big Ark pulled into second base, chest heaving and blowing like a porpoise, with a stand-up double. He stood on the bag and yelled at Stub in the batter's box.

"Get that mace around in there, Rook! Show us how they do it in the high-school leagues!"

Stub Alison grinned, then chuckled. How about that old pro out there? Just maybe a fellow named Alison responded to the needle, too.

Every pitcher had the rookie marked in his book as a pull hitter with power. They pitched him high and away, or low and tight on the fists. This time the Rebels' control must have slipped a little. The third pitch was waist high and just a little toward the outside edge of the strike zone. Stub was a split second late in swinging. He expected the ball to curve until the last instant. His bat came around in that natural, smooth, level cut.

Cra-a-ack!

A gray-white streak flashed past second base, ten feet off the ground and a little to the left of the bag.

Outfields played the rookie with center and right fielders pulled well around to the right and the left fielder a little shallow and nearly in his normal position. This drive drilled squarely into the yawning hole in the outer defense. The ball went to the wall, slanted off the barrier toward the flagpole in deep center field.

Stub turned first, steamed down to second while the center fielder chased the ball. He rounded the keystone sack. Country Selder leaped and waved his arms in the coaching box, beckoning the rookie on. Stub hit third base with his inside foot and dug deep for his last reserve of speed.

Everybody in the stadium was on his feet yelling for one side or the other. Teammates crowded the Goliath dugout lip, pounding, yelling, rooting the rookie home. Ark Molton stood ten feet beyond home plate with Layne beside him.

"Hit the dirt, kid, hit the dirt!" Molton yelled.

Rebel fielders handled the ball perfectly. Two fine throws from the deep corner and a sizzling peg from the shortstop in shallow left center. The ball hopped into the catcher's mitt the same instant as Stub started his slide.

The Rebel catcher had the base blocked. Stub's knee banged into an unyielding shin guard backed by two hundred pounds of braced bone and muscle. He was out by a wide margin. And of course it had to be the tender knee that he banged.

It was more than tender now, but he forced himself not to limp or grimace as he walked to the dugout and donned his gear.

The main thing was that the Goliaths were back on top, 3 to 2.

CHAPTER SIXTEEN

Bottom of the Ninth

Stub Alison crouched back of the plate for the bottom of the ninth inning. He felt a pulse hammer in the sore knee with every thump of his heart. He gritted his teeth. He had to last. There would be a long winter in which to rest the knee.

"We're going to take it," he muttered. "We've got to take it! Kendrick will make short work of these fellows!"

He knew deep down that it would not be that easy. They were going to have to win this game the hard way. The Rebels would make it nerve-shattering torture right down to the end.

The inner hunch proved all too accurate. Kendrick was working with no rest after the tension of yesterday's shutout win. Nobody ever accused the slick left-hander of lacking heart. But there must be physical capacity to back up the stoutest heart.

Kendrick worked a second strike on the leadoff batter after sneaking the first one through the strike zone, then losing the umpire's decision on a very close call. But Stub noted with sinking heart that Kendrick's fast ball had lost its zip. The curve he threw for the second pitch had hung a little, too. The fourth pitch was a hook that hardly broke at all. The batter cracked a screeching drive to right field good for two bases. The heat was on.

The southpaw worked hard on the next batter, maybe too hard. He tried to bend a curve in there on a three-and-two count and instead threw the ball into the dirt.

Stub flung himself desperately to block the wild pitch. The ball skittered through him a short distance. He pounced on it, cocked his arm. The Rebel on second did not try to advance. Country Selder came from the dugout. He looked questioningly at Stub. The catcher shrugged and gave his head a little shake.

"You're tiring pretty fast," Selder said to Kendrick. "I'm going to relieve you, but we'll talk as long as the umps will let us get away with it. It'll give the reliever a little longer to heat up."

"Who's coming in?" Stub asked.

Selder looked at him. "Who would you suggest?" Selder said curiously.

"Cagni. He can blow that fast ball past these guys!"

"It is Cagni." Selder nodded. "He's the best we have to shoot with, I figure."

The umpire in chief came from behind the plate. "Get someone in there if you're going to yank him, Selder," the arbiter said. "If you're leaving him in, let's go!"

Selder made an arm motion toward the bullpen. Cagni came through the gate, took his time walking in to the mound. Duke Kendrick stuffed his glove in his pocket and trudged head down toward the dugout. Fans gave him a near ovation which he richly deserved.

Two men on base, one in position to score the tying run on almost any safe hit. Last of the ninth, your team only one run to the good, and nobody out. What a spot for a rookie pitcher!

Stub's mind raced while he caught Cagni's range-finding pitches. Suddenly he recalled a play he had read about a Goliath catcher making many years ago when the Goliaths were one of the newest clubs in the league. The situation now was similar to the setup of that long-ago game. The stocky catcher carried the ball out to the mound after Cagni's final range-finding toss. The umpire had not yet called play.

"It's a cinch they'll try to sacrifice those runners along a base," Stub said. "The hitter may take one just to look it over. Bust it high but through there with plenty on it. Don't worry! I've got a plan to take the powder away from the Rebel guns!"

The stocky catcher clomped over to Schmidt. He called the third baseman out of earshot of the third-base coach.

"When I go back," Stub said, "shake your head as though you didn't agree with me. Play deep. *Don't try to field a bunt, just cover the sack!*"

Schmidt started to protest.

"I'll take the responsibility," Stub shut him off. A wry grin lifted his lips. "The newspapers would give me the discredit anyway if things went sour. But you'd look awful bad if I buzzed a throw down here and you weren't covering!"

The rookie catcher watched the batter closely as Cagni took his stretch and delivered. He felt a satisfaction at seeing the Rebel relax and shorten his grip. He was up there to bunt, all right. Probably had orders from his manager to dump the first good pitch. The high, fast one did not appeal to him, but the umpire ruled it a strike. That was good. The batter would not let another good one pass.

"Hang tough out there!" Stub yelled to Cagni. "Gun that rock in here. Don't waste any on this guy!"

He signed for a letter-high fast ball, a perfect pitch to bunt. He was careful to wait until the ball had left Cagni's hand and was halfway to the plate. The rules forbade a catcher leaving the catcher's box until after the pitcher delivered the ball. Then, saying a silent prayer to the baseball gods, the rookie catcher dashed from his place behind the plate and leaped down the third-base line!

There was absolutely nothing to stop the ball from going to the stands if the batter didn't hit it!

Up in the press box Milt Binkley cried, "Oh, no! What a way to lose a World Championship!" Binkley closed his eyes and missed the greatest, most daring play in all the years he had covered baseball.

The sign had been passed from his bench. The batter had his eye on the ball and his bat ready to poke the pitch. He poked it—right into the big mitt of Stub Alison on the first bound ten feet from the plate in fair ground.

Stub whirled and rifled the ball to Schmidt, standing with one foot anchored to the bag. The veteran third baseman caught the ball and practically in the same motion whipped a throw to Monk Banyan. Banyan kicked the second-base bag and his hard throw to Ark Molton barely missed nipping the man who had made the bunt!

A near triple play but a positive double play. On a perfect sacrifice bunt. Silence held the great crowd a long moment. Then a great roar exploded.

Milt Binkley opened his eyes at the roar. He blinked dazedly at seeing two Rebels walking dejectedly from the diamond.

"What happened?" he demanded hoarsely. "What kept those runners from both scoring on the passed ball?"

"Passed ball, my eye! You missed the nerviest, smartest rally-killing play this man's ball park ever saw!"

Jake Dahl had watched the Series from the press box. The veteran backstop nearly rebroke his bad finger again pounding a table on which Binkley's typewriter rested.

"Another Goliath catcher pulled that play a hundred years ago," Dahl said. "Give or take a few years! Old Chuck Ginzelle. It takes guts in the clutch! There isn't one catcher in a thousand with the brains and guts to pull a play like that! But the kid did it—and if he hasn't won the Series for us, I'll eat your typewriter!"

Cagni blew down the next batter with three smoking fast balls.

WORLD CHAMPIONS!
The Goliaths had capped their grueling comeback

with the fightingest finish the Series ever witnessed. Such
a club truly richly deserved the hard-won title, World
Champions!

Stub Alison sat on a bench in the dressing room slowly
taking off his uniform. He wondered what Country Selder
and several veterans were talking so earnestly about across
the room.

Better get showered and dressed before Selder opened
the door and all the newspaper people stormed in. A
grimace of pain wrenched the youngster as he pulled the
stocking off his right leg.

Maybe Selder had something, he thought. Maybe a
fellow would last a lot longer in the outfield. But an outfielder could get plunked by a pitch ball. Oh, well, catcher
or outfield, this being a big leaguer is—

Stub broke off his thoughts and stared bewildered at the
gang of grinning, husky ballplayers abruptly in front of
him. Suddenly Ark Molton lunged at him.

"Take the fighting little banty rooster!" Ark yelled.

The burly first baseman pinioned the rookie's arms.
Clancy and Fox each grabbed a leg. Banyan and Schmidt
peeled off his shirt and sliding pads. Before he realized
what was happening, Stub was under a shower. Ark Molton turned on the water.

"What goes on?" Stub sputtered. "You big apes! I'll—
splff—ye—ou—ou!"

He gasped as the spray of the cold shower drove the
breath from his lungs. Almost immediately Big Mike
Clancy and Ark Molton hustled him from under the water.

Molton grabbed a big towel and wrapped it around the rookie's shoulders.

"He ought to be cooled enough to listen good now, Lefty," Molton said. "Do your stuff."

Lefty Byrnes stood before the catcher, one hand behind him.

"I'm speaking for all of us," Lefty began. "Country and Ark have wised us up to the real business back of your needling. Guess maybe we should have seen what your razzing did for us. Anyway, we want you to know that we appreciate the way your blasted, razor-edged cracks made us play ball. We want you to know that from now on you're one of us."

The pitcher's eyes twinkled and he gripped something in the hand behind him a little tighter.

"We hereby initiate you as a full member in good standing of the Veterans of Baseball Wars. Lacking a bottle of champagne to crack over your head, we can't do it proper. But we christen you—"

Wh—is—sh!

Byrnes whanged the paper bag of water he had held over Alison's head, and the gang of veterans yelled:

"WORLD CHAMPION ROOKIE!"

That was the signal for hilarity. Suddenly the Goliath dressing room was a madhouse. These hard-shell veterans acted like a pack of high school kids who had just won the county championship.

Stub gazed dumfounded at Big Mike and Ark Molton doing an impromptu jitter-bug dance. Fox pummeled the youngster in the ribs and slapped him on the shoulder.

"You're aces, kid, with all of us," Fox said. "You know, looking back, some of your cracks were really funny." Fox chuckled.

"That thing you pulled on me, running bases like crazy on an out-of-the-park homer, was quite a stunt. But that thing you pulled today! Kid, there sure was nothing funny about *that* stunt!"

Stub looked at the wiry shortstop. He looked again at Big Mike and Molton jumping around like overgrown kids. He caught Country Selder's eye, and suddenly the thought that had been in his mind when they ganged him returned.

He grinned at Country Selder.

"You know something?" the youngster asked. "Catcher or outfielder, this being a big leaguer just can't be matched!"

Stub Alison grinned widely and added in a soft Georgia drawl, "You hear!"